**"How am I supposed to conduct my investigation when I have to spend all my time worrying about you?"**

His face was mere inches from hers, his blue eyes smoky and intense.

"You don't—" she started, but her voice was swallowed up by the pounding of her heart. "You don't have to worry about me."

He touched her bruised neck with a surprisingly gentle fingertip. "Look at this. Of course I have to worry. If something happened to you I'd—"

Anna raised her head, meeting his gaze. His eyes lingered on her lips as his fingers slid around the back of her neck.

She melted inside, overwhelmed by his gentle touch, his quiet, caring words, the naked yearning in his eyes.

Reality tried to break the spell his tenderness had cast. *Not him,* her brain scolded. Not Texas Ranger Zane McKinney. She had every reason to hate him and no reason at all to trust him. She pulled away from his hypnotic touch.

"I'd better get back to my room."

"You're not going anywhere. I can't trust you out of my sight, so you're sleeping here."

# MALLORY KANE

# SIX-GUN INVESTIGATION

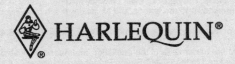

TORONTO • NEW YORK • LONDON
AMSTERDAM • PARIS • SYDNEY • HAMBURG
STOCKHOLM • ATHENS • TOKYO • MILAN • MADRID
PRAGUE • WARSAW • BUDAPEST • AUCKLAND

To Delores and Rita—
silver stars in their own right!

ISBN-13: 978-0-373-88739-2
ISBN-10: 0-373-88739-6

SIX-GUN INVESTIGATION

www.eHarlequin.com

**Printed in U.S.A.**

## ABOUT THE AUTHOR

Mallory Kane took early retirement from her position as assistant chief of pharmacy at a large metropolitan medical center to pursue her other loves, writing and art. She has published and won awards for science fiction and fantasy as well as romance. Mallory credits her love of books to her mother, who taught her that books are a precious resource and should be treated with loving respect. Her grandfather and her father were both steeped in the Southern tradition of oral history, and could hold an audience spellbound with their storytelling skills. Mallory aspires to be as good a storyteller as her father. She loves romantic suspense with dangerous heroes and dauntless heroines. She is also fascinated by story ideas that explore the infinite capacity of the brain to adapt and develop higher skills.

Mallory lives in Mississippi with her husband and their cat. She would be delighted to hear from readers. You can write to her c/o Harlequin Books, 233 Broadway, Suite 1001, New York, NY 10279.

## Books by Mallory Kane

HARLEQUIN INTRIGUE

*Ultimate Agents

# CAST OF CHARACTERS

**Zane McKinney**—A Texas Ranger who's risen to the top of his field. But no accolades can make up for his father's betrayal. Now, with a woman dead and his father once again the prime suspect, Zane will do anything to find the truth—anything except fall in love with the daughter of the woman who destroyed his family.

**Anna Wallace**—Sixteen years ago, this investigative journalist's mother was murdered in the small town of Justice, Texas. Now her sister is dead by the same hand, and the only man who can help her find the murderer is the son of the suspected killer.

**Sarah Wallace**—Sarah begged Anna to meet in Justice, claiming she had proof of who had killed Lou Ann.

**Jim McKinney**—The ex-Texas Ranger's career and life were destroyed when his mistress was found strangled to death.

**Stella McKinney**—Jim's long-suffering wife. Does Stella know more than she's telling?

**Leland Hendricks**—When his trophy wife's daughter is murdered, this wheeler-dealer has an airtight alibi.

**Donna Hendricks**—A reformed alcoholic, Donna lost custody of her toddler son to her ex-husband, Leland. Then the child went missing.

**Rosa Buchanan**—Employee and confidante of Donna, Rosa would do anything for her friend.

# Prologue

For the third time in fifteen minutes, Sarah Wallace reached for her purse—for the cigarettes that weren't there. She'd quit smoking two weeks ago. Two weeks, and yet she still reached for them whenever she was nervous.

*Damn.* How would she last for eight more months? She sighed and glanced at the half-eaten sandwich she'd ordered up to her room from the diner next door to the Matheson Inn. *Ugh.* It had tasted good, but now it sat heavily on her queasy stomach. She dumped the container into the wastebasket and snagged a piece of sugarless gum with the tips of her silk nails.

"I'm doing all this for you, kid," she whispered as she chewed. Her left hand drifted to her flat tummy. "I'm working on getting rid of the crap in my life, so you and I can start fresh. I've got a feeling the cigarettes were easy, compared to the rest."

Then she turned back to the sheet of hotel paper lying on the desk. Picking up the pen, she quickly read over what she'd written.

*Dear Anna,*

*I'm sitting in this room in Justice, wondering if I'm doing the right thing. It feels right. But here, in the same room where Mom was murdered, I'm beginning to feel a little spooked. Silly, I know, but if you don't get here very soon I may chicken out and leave.*

*Hopefully within a few minutes we'll be reading this together and laughing at my paranoia.*

She underlined paranoia three times. She'd gotten a few curious looks when she'd shown up. Hadn't seen anyone she knew but that didn't mean someone hadn't seen her.

She wrote the last lines quickly, and finished with a plea she'd be able to deliver in person in a few minutes.

*Hey, Anna-banana, I'm so sorry I left you. I hope you can forgive me. I want us to get past Mom's deathand be a family. We can drink a toast—a non-alcoholic toast—to new beginnings.*

She smiled as she signed the note and put it in the safest place she knew, where she and Anna had so often hidden notes to each other.

"Well, kid." She patted her tummy. Writing the note made her feel better. The apprehension that had squeezed her chest since the moment she'd found out she was pregnant faded.

She glanced at the fake Rolex on her wrist. "Now if your aunt Anna would hurry up and get here…"

It had been weird, talking to her baby sister after all these years. Anna had been cautious and reserved, and with good reason. Sarah had bailed on her after their mother's murder and headed for Las Vegas. She couldn't blame Anna for doubting that now, sixteen years later, Sarah regretted abandoning her.

Anna hadn't even wanted to talk to her, much less meet her in Justice, Texas, where their mother had been murdered—that is until Sarah told her what she'd found.

After a dumbstruck pause, Anna had reluctantly agreed.

"She should be here by now," Sarah muttered, reaching for her purse. Her hand clenched in a fist. *No cigarettes,* she reminded herself sternly. *You don't smoke.*

She paced instead, working the gum until her jaw ached.

Maybe Anna was right. Maybe this was a stupid idea, coming back to the scene of the crime, so to speak. A frisson of anxiety slid up her spine at the memory of what had happened to her mother in this very room.

She should have followed her first instinct and met Anna in Dallas. *But no.* She had to make a big production out of it. Blame Lou Ann's flair for the dramatic, which Sarah had obviously inherited and Anna had not.

Tossing the now flavorless gum into the wastebasket, she stepped over to the window, carefully skirting the area of the floor where their mother had been found on a night like tonight, strangled with her own purse strap.

She peered out through the heavy curtains. It had gotten dark. She cursed under her breath. She'd been in Justice for three hours, and that was two hours and fifty-nine minutes too long. Just as soon as she turned everything over to Anna, she'd be out of here, one more load of crap lighter.

A sharp rap on the door startled her.

"Thank God!" Anna was finally here. Sarah rushed over and opened the door.

Her heart jumped into her throat when she saw who was standing there.

"You!" she blurted.

"It's been a long time, Sarah. May I come in?"

Sarah held on to the door. "I suppose I can guess who told you I was here."

"You know what small towns are like. Nobody can keep a secret."

"You certainly managed. Go away. I have nothing to say to you." Sarah took a step backward to push the door closed.

"Hold it. What are you doing here?"

"None of your business. Now leave me alone." She pushed again, but suddenly the heavy wooden door slammed into her, banging her head and knocking her on her butt.

She scrambled to her feet, slightly dazed, but before she could straighten, pain exploded in her head.

Sarah cradled her belly protectively as everything went black.

## Chapter One

Lieutenant Zane McKinney, Texas Ranger, entered the Matheson Inn and stepped into the middle of chaos. The dozen or more people crowded into the small lobby parted like the Red Sea as he stalked toward the registration desk. He felt their eyes on him—surprised and curious. He heard their whispered questions and comments.

*What's Zane McKinney doing here?*

*Never thought he'd set foot in Justice again. Always was too good for this town.*

*Reckon he's here about the murder?*

He ignored the whispers and glared at the slouchy desk clerk who seemed oblivious to the crowd, then he turned around, letting his gaze slide over the familiar faces.

"Get on home, folks. There's nothing to see here."

The thing about small towns, everybody knew everybody else's business. It was going to be hard to take charge over former neighbors and high school buddies.

"Zane." Tommy Driver stepped up and stuck out his hand. "Been a long time. What's happening? Is that really Lou Ann Wallace's girl in there?"

Zane shook Tommy's hand. His dad owned the hardware store and he'd been a basketball star back in high school. "Do me a favor, Tom. Help me clear out the lobby. They're contaminating the crime scene."

"It is her, ain't it? Are you in charge?"

Zane sent Tommy a look, and the tall former basketball player turned toward the crowd and held up his hands. "Come on, y'all. We might as well go home. Zane McKinney's here now. Everything's under control."

Zane heard the thinly veiled sarcasm in Tommy's voice. As several gasps and a few chuckles rippled through the crowd, he nodded at Tommy, then addressed the desk clerk. "Don't let anybody else in. Nobody! Got it?"

"No problem, dude," the twenty-something kid with his thick neck and buzz haircut muttered.

Zane surveyed the lobby as he kept one eye on the people slowly dispersing. The dark polished wood of the floors and staircase lent a rich look to the old mansion that had been converted into an inn long before Zane was born.

There, down the hall beside the stairs, was Room One, the most infamous room in the Matheson Inn—the room where Lou Ann Wallace Hendricks had been murdered sixteen years before.

Now the room would be an even bigger tourist attraction. Now it would be known as the place where Lou Ann *and* her daughter Sarah had both died.

With a last look around to be sure everyone had cleared out, he walked down the hall and stepped into more chaos. There were at least eight people in the room, not counting the dead body. And that was seven too many.

Annoyed, Zane swiftly cataloged the occupants.

The mayor and Leland Hendricks were standing near the bathroom door with their heads together.

Dr. Jonathan Evans, the only man who should have been there, was kneeling on the floor beside the body.

A young Hispanic man dressed in a T-shirt and sweatpants was taking photographs with a digital camera.

And on the far side of the room, sitting alone and rigid in a desk chair, was a pale young woman who looked familiar.

Zane heard keys jangling behind him. It was the desk clerk. He slouched in the doorway staring at the corpse with lewd interest. Beyond him in the hall, a couple of young teen boys hung back, trying to get a peek at the shocking scene.

"All right, folks," Zane said. He didn't raise his voice, but every eye turned toward him.

The mayor headed his way, with Hendricks following. The guy holding the camera froze. Dr. Evans glanced up, nodded slightly, then went back to his examination.

"I want everybody out of here." Zane turned toward the boys lurking at the door. "Starting with you two. Go home."

The two boys backed away, then turned and ran.

"You." He pointed at the clerk. "What did I tell you? Get back to the desk. Lock the doors. Don't let anyone in or out. And get me a master key."

The clerk ran his hand over his bristly hair, and the keys started jangling again. He muttered something unintelligible as he slouched out of the room.

"Zane." The mayor stuck out his hand. "I was surprised when your captain told me he was sending you, considering…"

"Mayor, Leland, step outside please. This is a crime scene."

The mayor frowned. Hendricks smirked and took another step toward Zane. "I'm not leaving. I need to be here with my stepdaughter—"

Zane met his gaze. "Now."

A slow flush rose up Hendricks's neck to his face and he opened his mouth, but the mayor laid a hand on his arm.

"Come on, Leland. We'll leave *Lieutenant McKinney* to do his job."

Leland Hendricks shook off the mayor's hand and walked over to the young woman perched on the chair. He whispered something to her and she nodded.

But Zane, who'd spent his career teaching himself to observe everything from body language to eye movements, noticed the quickly masked moue of distaste that crossed her face.

Zane waited until the mayor and Hendricks were gone. He cursed silently. The whole damn inn, including the scene of the murder, was thoroughly contaminated by now.

When Captain Hardy had called an hour

before and ordered him to take charge of a murder and attempted murder in Justice, Texas, Zane had been stunned. Not only had a woman been murdered, Sheriff Matheson had been wounded while in pursuit of a possible suspect.

Zane's shock was well-founded. Nothing ever happened in his hometown—not that he'd know from personal experience. He hadn't been here recently. He lived in Garland, and while technically Justice was part of his territory, he'd managed to avoid returning to the town where his father lived in disgrace.

But the murder wasn't the biggest shock—that honor belonged to the victim. It was Sarah Wallace, the daughter of the only other adult who'd been murdered in Justice in the past forty years—Lou Ann Wallace Hendricks. Zane's gut clenched at the thought of the woman who'd ripped his family apart in life and in death.

Zane had hung up from his captain and immediately called the mayor with specific instructions to keep everyone except Dr. Evans away from the scene of the murder.

But good luck keeping anything quiet in a place like Justice. Another in the long list of reasons he'd sworn never to come back to his hometown.

He stepped closer to the body, examining the familiar face, discolored and contorted in death. Sarah Wallace looked just like her mother. Same brassy-bleached hair, same overdone makeup, same too tight, too flashy clothes.

His lips thinned in disapproval and aversion. Just like her mother in life and just like her in death.

He'd been away at college when Lou Ann was killed. The most memorable thing about her death was that his father, Jim McKinney, had been indicted.

Only the presence of more than one semen sample in Lou Ann's body and the double-talk of a slick Dallas lawyer had kept him from serving time. The evidence was ruled insufficient to convict. But for Zane, it was more than enough.

"Who're you?" he asked the man holding the camera.

"Deputy Sheriff Luis Spinoza." Spinoza straightened a bit. "I was in bed when the call came."

Zane nodded. "Give me the camera. Why didn't you kick the mayor and Hendricks out?" The question was a waste of air. He read the answer in the young man's face. Just the thought of confronting the mayor of

Justice or its most prominent citizen had him cowed.

Zane sighed. "Never mind. Who's processing the second crime scene?"

"Uh, nobody—sir. That is, not yet. Deputy Enis rode in the ambulance with Carley— uh—Sheriff Matheson—over to Calhoun City, to County General."

"Call him. Get him back here. The sheriff's in good hands, and we need the manpower here. Got another camera?"

The deputy nodded. "Back at the office."

"Did you bring a kit? Crime scene tape?"

"Right over there." He pointed to a stainless steel case beside the door.

"Good. Tape off the door to this room. Leave me the kit. I assume you have another one."

The deputy nodded eagerly. "Lieutenant, should I call our other deputy, Burns?"

"You've got a third deputy? Where's he tonight?"

"He's supposed to be on vacation. He's building a deck on his house."

"Call him. Then go secure the area where the sheriff was shot and process it." Zane looked the deputy up and down. "You do know how to process a crime scene, don't you?"

Spinoza straightened even more and his cheeks flushed. "Yes, sir."

"Get going then." He glanced around the room. "Hold it a second, Deputy."

Spinoza turned back.

"Has anyone touched anything? That suitcase? The handbag?"

"No, sir. I kept an eye on them."

"Excellent." Zane nodded dismissively and turned his attention to the doctor.

Dr. Jonathan Evans sat back on his haunches and raised his eyes to meet Zane's. "Lieutenant. Been a while."

Zane dipped his head in acknowledgment. He and Jon had graduated from high school the same year.

"Hard to believe, isn't it? That she was killed here in the same room where her mother was murdered?"

Zane took in the dead woman's discolored face and the puddle of blood under her head.

"Yeah." He'd gotten over the initial shock. Now he was assessing the scene like an investigator, and his first thought was that his dad was probably the prime suspect, just like he had been sixteen years ago. And knowing his dad, his alibi wouldn't be any more credible than it was back then.

"Did you get a chance to check out Carley's wounds?"

The doctor shook his head. "Nope. I came straight here. Spinoza called me. He's a good man."

"Glad to hear it. What do you know about Carley's injury?"

"I called the Emergency Room staff physician myself. Told him to preserve any evidence he finds on her."

"The slug?"

"Through and through."

*Damn.* "Did he say how she's doing?"

"Apparently it was a flesh wound in her side, but it may have nicked a rib. If that's the case, she'll be out of commission for a few days."

"Thanks, Jon." Zane turned his attention to the dead woman. "COD?"

"My best guess is that the cause of death was strangulation. She's got petechial hemorrhaging in her eyes."

"What about all the blood?"

"Blunt force trauma to the left side of the head, premortem. Too much blood for it to have been inflicted after death."

"Spatter?"

"Over there by the door. Some of it has already been smeared by onlookers."

Zane cursed under his breath. "What about TOD?"

"From the appearance of the blood and her liver temp, I'd say she died some time between seven and seven-thirty. We should know precisely when we get the autopsy results."

Zane pulled a pair of exam gloves out of his pocket and started to kneel beside the body, but a small sound from behind him reminded him that there was one other person in the room who needed his attention. He stuck the gloves back into his pocket.

*Anna Wallace.* Annie. He turned, and for an instant his vision wavered and he saw the gawky, mousy-haired teenager with glasses and braces who, unlike her mother and older sister, had always been serious and subdued.

He wondered if he'd have even remembered her if his captain hadn't told him she'd be here. He'd been a senior in high school when Lou Ann Wallace had shown up in town with her two daughters. Sarah was his age, and a younger, flashier version of her mother.

Annie had been a sophomore, or maybe a freshman—a kid not worthy of a second look by a senior.

Then when their mother was killed, Zane had been in school at the University of Texas. Thinking of Lou Ann made Zane think of his dad. He shook off the depressing thoughts and made a mental note to get the records of Lou Ann's murder.

"Annie Wallace?" he said gently.

She hadn't taken her eyes off her sister since he'd walked into the room. From her position perched like a nervous bird on the edge of the desk chair clutching the long strap of her purse, she had a clear view of Sarah's face.

Zane touched her shoulder lightly. "Annie?"

With an obvious effort, she shut her eyes for an instant, then looked up at him.

No glasses now. Her eyes were a deep olive-green and wide with shock in her colorless face. Her dark hair was twisted up and held by some kind of barrette, and she didn't have on any makeup, at least none he could see.

"It's Anna."

"Sorry. It's been a long time. Weren't you called Annie in school?"

She nodded jerkily and put a hand to her throat. "You're Zane McKinney."

It wasn't a question, so he didn't bother to answer. The mayor had told him she'd found her sister's body. It stood to reason he'd have told Anna that Zane would be taking over the investigation.

*Ironic,* considering—

Stopping his brain from going down that path, he knelt beside her chair. "I need to ask you some questions."

Her eyes flickered toward the awkwardly sprawled body of her sister and her hands tightened on the strap of the bag that hung from her shoulder.

"Have you been processed? I mean, has anyone—"

"I know what it means," she said shortly. Her voice quivered slightly, but all in all it was stronger and steadier than he'd expected it to be. After all, she'd apparently walked in and found her sister murdered in the exact same way her mother had been sixteen years before. He wondered if she'd seen her mother lying here.

"No. I haven't been processed." She moistened her lips. "Do you want to do that now?"

Zane rose and stepped backward. "Yeah. Let's get it out of the way. Step out into the hall."

"What about Sarah?"

"Dr. Evans will take good care of her." He

moved so that he blocked Anna's view of her sister's body.

He'd dealt with distraught family members before, but he didn't think he'd ever seen anyone who'd worked as hard as Anna Wallace was working right now to hold herself together.

She was doing a good job of it, but something about her slender bowed shoulders, the determined set of her jaw and her haunted eyes tugged at a place deep inside him, a sore place. Could it be his heart?

*Ha.* If anyone asked the people in Justice—especially his own family—they'd probably deny that Zane McKinney had a heart.

Anna stood in a stiff, wobbly motion.

He reached out and touched her lower back to steady her. She was only a few inches shorter than his six feet one. She'd grown since high school.

His eyes quickly took in every inch of her. She'd grown a *lot*. He did the math in his head. When he was eighteen, she'd been fifteen, much too young to interest a senior. But now he was thirty-four, she was thirty-one. Hell, they were practically the same age.

She looked at him quizzically and he

realized his mind had wandered. *Damn.* That never happened to him.

"Are you staying with Leland?" he asked.

"No."

Her answer was quick. Too quick.

"I mean, I wasn't planning to stay at all—" Her eyes flitted back toward her sister's body.

"Okay. Why don't I get you a room? You stand right there and don't move." He pulled out his cell phone.

"Could you—"

He looked up.

"Could you ask them to make it on a different floor?"

Zane knew he had a heart, because it squeezed in compassion at her quiet request. He nodded. "Jon, do you know the number of the front desk?"

The doctor rattled it off and Zane quickly secured a room on the second floor.

"Let's go." He touched the small of her back again and led her to the door, snagging the processing kit as he passed it.

Just as they ducked under the crime scene tape that the deputy had draped haphazardly across the doorway, a pair of shiny tooled-leather cowboy boots appeared in Zane's line of sight.

*Ah, hell.* He knew those boots. They had to be thirty years old, but they shone like new.

He composed his face and straightened, pulling Anna just a bit closer. Then he steeled himself and looked into the blue-gray eyes that were unnervingly like his own.

"Hello, son," Jim McKinney said.

Zane's throat constricted and his scalp burned with a swift and unreasoning anger.

*Typical.* If there was trouble involving a female, Gentleman Jim would be right in the middle of it.

"What the hell are you doing here?" he asked, concentrating on not balling his hands into fists.

Jim took off his pearl-gray Stetson with one hand and took Anna's hand with the other. "Anna, I'm so sorry about your sister." He bent his head and formally kissed her fingers.

Zane's internal pressure gauge was about to blow. He wanted to shove his father away from Anna. He took a step forward. "This is a crime scene. Get out."

Jim frowned at him, then looked beyond him into the room. "I thought I could help out, what with poor Carley in the hospital. Didn't know the Rangers were sending you."

"Well, now you do. And you also know I don't need any help."

Jim cocked one eyebrow. "Especially not from me, right?"

Zane inclined his head. He couldn't be angry with the desk clerk for allowing his father inside. There wasn't a soul in Justice who would deny ex-Texas Ranger Jim McKinney access to a crime scene. He was pissed at himself for letting his old man make him feel like a rookie.

"On second thought, where were you between seven and seven-thirty tonight?"

A shadow of shock and pain crossed Jim McKinney's weathered face. But he recovered quickly and grinned. "Everybody's a suspect."

"Not everybody," Zane muttered, feeling mean.

"I was home eating dinner."

Zane made a disgusted sound. "At seven? Since when do y'all eat that late?"

Jim's back straightened as a slight flush stained his cheeks. "Since I started working at the supermarket in Calhoun City. This week I'm on the day shift. I get off at six-thirty. It takes a good half hour to drive home."

A pang hit Zane underneath his breastbone. Jim McKinney, working at a supermarket.

His dad had been a highly decorated Ranger until that day back in 1991 when a desk clerk at the Matheson Inn had found Lou Ann Wallace strangled to death. He'd resigned from the force under a cloud of suspicion. Since then he'd fought with depression and the tendency to drown his sorrows in a bottle, and he'd had trouble keeping a job.

Clamping his jaw, Zane pushed away the crippling sympathy for the man he'd once idolized. There was no place in this investigation for emotions. He was the chief investigator, and just like sixteen years ago, Jim McKinney was a suspect.

"I thought I'd see if there was anything I could do to help."

Zane glared at him. "Well, there's not. I'll get your statement later. Right now I've got to take care of Annie."

Jim McKinney's eyes crinkled and his lips curved into a sympathetic smile as he turned his attention back to Anna. "Again, if there's anything I can do—"

"Thank you, Mr. McKinney," she said quietly.

Jim started past them toward Room One. His back was slightly bowed and he was turning gray at the temples. He was only fifty-seven.

Zane winced. When had his dad gotten old?

He clenched his jaw. "Dad, I meant it. You can't go in there. Get out of here."

Jim sent him a sharp look. "I'll tell your mother you'll be by to see her."

"You do that." Zane heard the ice in his voice. Sometimes he felt like it ran through his veins, too. But cool detachment and focused determination worked for him. As a Ranger, especially a lieutenant, he couldn't afford to lose his objectivity. For Zane, being a good Ranger was job one.

As his dad's boots echoed on the hardwood floor, Anna turned to look back toward the room.

Zane wrapped his arm a little more tightly around her waist. He didn't want her looking at her sister's purple contorted face again. He couldn't afford to have her break down before he had a chance to question her.

In Room Four on the second floor, he set the crime scene case on the bed and opened it, then retrieved a pair of exam gloves from his pocket and pulled them on. He took out a portable fingerprint kit and several swabs.

Without looking up, he spoke. "Tell me what happened."

Anna watched in fascination as Zane's gloved fingers laid out the forensic tools on the bed. His hands were sturdy yet graceful, like the rest of him. He moved efficiently, no wasted effort.

She raised her gaze to his face. His even features and high cheekbones made him classically handsome. His mouth was wide and straight and there was a tiny bump on his nose where he must have broken it. It was his only flaw, unless she counted the tense muscle that bulged in his jaw. The muscle that had popped out when they'd run into his father.

"Annie?"

She blinked. He'd asked her something. People kept talking to her, but her thoughts were scattered. She couldn't focus. The rational part of her brain knew she was suffering from shock. As a journalist, she'd talked to enough people in a similar state that she recognized the symptoms. But knowing what was wrong didn't help her shake it.

She'd listened to the mayor, to Leland, to the doctor and the deputy sheriff, but right now she couldn't remember what any of them had said.

She did remember Jim McKinney kissing her hand. He'd always been a charmer. He loved women, and apparently many of them found it hard to resist his rugged good looks, including her mother. She couldn't help but wonder why he'd shown up. Was it to see his son, or did it have to do with her sister?

Her chest constricted painfully and she twisted the leather strap of her purse around her fingers. Sarah was dead, just like her mother, and Jim McKinney could have killed her.

"Annie, I know it's hard, but I need you to work with me." Zane's voice was calm and smooth, yet compelling, like his manner. As soon as he'd walked into Sarah's room, the whole atmosphere had changed. He was in charge and everyone knew it.

"Tell me what happened," he repeated.

She sent him an assessing glance. Apparently her journalist instincts hadn't completely quit working. He might appear solicitous and gentle, but in the few seconds she'd been watching him, her brain had already figured out two things.

His hawklike eyes missed nothing, and he had serious issues with his father. There was another dynamic at work here, as well. In her career, she'd learned to read people pretty well. It was a skill she'd honed carefully over the past few years.

Lieutenant Zane McKinney, Texas Ranger, was not happy to be back in his hometown.

Not at all. And furthermore, at least two people—the mayor and her stepfather—were not happy to have him back.

"Do you want me to ask Dr. Evans to give you a tranquilizer?"

"No." She almost laughed. The last thing she wanted was to be drugged. She needed a clear head. It was going to take all her intuition and skill to answer this man's questions without making him suspicious.

She struggled to focus on his questions. "I'm fine. You want to know what happened when I found Sarah?"

"Why don't we start from the beginning? Why did you and Sarah come back here, to the same room where your mother was murdered?"

Zane's words ripped through Anna like a knife. "The same room! Oh, my God! I'd forgotten." Sarah had told her the room number, but she hadn't made the connection.

Still, it made sense. "My sister always was a drama queen—" Her voice broke a little. She cleared her throat, irritated at herself for giving in to her emotions.

Taking a deep breath, she fought the vague nausea that clung to her. She hadn't seen her sister since she was sixteen. How could it hurt so much that she was dead?

She swallowed acrid saliva. "Do you see a glass? I could use some water." She sat down on the edge of the double bed.

Zane raised an eyebrow, then turned on his booted heel and wasting no motion, took two long strides into the bathroom. The water ran briefly, then he was back.

She took the glass from his big elegant hand and sipped it slowly. The cool liquid soothed her throat, which was raw from the bitter nausea that had threatened to erupt ever since she'd walked in and seen Sarah sprawled on that floor.

Zane stood over her, his impatience palpable. "Done?" he asked, holding out his hand for the glass.

She took another swallow.

"Anna, I need to process you," he said firmly. "I need to hear your account of what happened. And I don't have a lot of time. I've still got two crime scenes to oversee."

She handed him the glass and he set it down on the bedside table. That last mouthful had been hard to force past the lump in her throat anyway.

"I'm sorry. Why was Sarah here? I really have no idea. We haven't spoken since she took her portion of my mother's life insurance and left town. Then yesterday she called me. Asked me to meet her." She looked up at him, presenting what she called her concerned journalist face.

His eyes bore right through her. "Did she say why?"

She picked up the glass, looking at it instead of him as she lied to him. "No."

That wasn't as hard as she'd thought it would be. Running a finger around the rim of the glass, she took a long breath and met his gaze. "All she said was she wanted to start a new life."

A hollow, sickening sense of loss hit her in the solar plexus, the worst one yet. It surprised her how alone she suddenly felt.

She'd never gotten over the aching resentment toward Sarah for abandoning her. After their mother's death, Sarah hadn't wasted any time getting out of here. She'd left Anna with Leland Hendricks, a stepfather she hardly knew.

"I don't believe you."

Those words, spoken calmly and quietly, sent fear skittering along her nerve endings. She looked at Zane's hands, which were peeling the backing off a sheet of fingerprint paper. They were big, competent and graceful, like him.

Her gaze slid up the front of his white dress

shirt, past the Texas Ranger badge and the stylish tie to his face. What would it take to satisfy him? How much of the truth did she dare reveal?

She took a long breath and nodded. "Okay. Sarah said she had some information for me."

Zane stepped over to the old-fashioned desk near the window. "Come sit over here."

Anna complied. "My fingerprints are on file," she said. "They were taken when my mother died."

He didn't answer that. "Hold out your hands."

She did, noticing that they trembled.

"It's okay, Annie. We'll be done here soon."

There was that smooth, low voice again. She was going to have to watch herself around him. Something about that voice and those eyes made her want to trust him, put all the burden on his strong, capable shoulders. But she didn't dare. Not until she knew more.

As he took her fingers one by one and pressed them onto the sticky paper, she studied him.

She remembered him from high school. Who wouldn't? He'd been the best-looking boy in Justice. During his senior year, he'd ruled the school. Valedictorian, Mr. JHS, quarterback for the district championship football team—and who knew what else. He'd always been too good for such a small town.

His deep golden-brown hair was a little long for a Ranger, at least the Rangers she'd come in contact with in Dallas. The years had been good to him—very good. He looked more like his father than he had at eighteen. Age and experience had given his pretty-boy face character. There was no doubt he'd still hold his own as the best-looking guy in town.

"What exactly did Sarah say to you about information?"

His question startled her. She'd almost been lulled into thinking he was done. She should have known better.

"She told me she was sorry she'd left me alone. Said she wanted to start a new life, and that she had some information I might find useful."

He finished with the fingerprints and lifted his head. "What kind of information?"

"I don't know." It was all she could do not to look away from his intense smoky gaze.

"Why didn't she tell you on the phone?"

He still held her left hand. She pulled it away. "She said she wanted to see me." Tears stung her eyes but she blinked them away.

He carefully replaced the backing on the fingerprint paper and labeled it.

"Was that it, or was it because the information she had she couldn't just tell you?"

"What do you mean?"

"Maybe she wanted to see you, not to tell you something, but to give you something."

Anna shook her head. "I don't know why you'd think that."

"Why the same room?" he asked again.

"I told you. I don't know. She called yesterday, around five o'clock. She asked me to meet her here this evening at seven."

Zane took a PDA from his shirt pocket and made a note.

"I got caught in traffic, so I was late—" Her breath caught.

*Concentrate,* she lectured herself, clenching her fists. She was a journalist. She knew better than to allow her emotions to overtake her objectivity. She had to treat this as just another story. She couldn't get caught up in grief or regret. There was too much at stake.

She'd tried to resist her sister's urgent plea, tried to make herself believe that Sarah was exaggerating when she said she had proof of who'd killed their mother.

In fact, she'd almost talked herself into not coming at all. That's why she'd been late. And her indecision had cost her sister her life.

Tears pricked her eyelids as she looked up

at Zane. He was watching her carefully. "If I'd gotten here earlier, Sarah might still be alive."

He lifted a hand as if to reach for hers, but checked the movement and rested it on the table instead. His sharp gaze bored through her. He took a deep breath.

"If you'd gotten here earlier, you'd have died, too."

## Chapter Two

Zane watched with a mixture of satisfaction and guilt as the last bit of color drained from Anna's face.

*Good.* At least he'd broken through that thick barrier of self-control for a second. He needed to retain the upper hand.

Anna Wallace was hiding something behind those olive-green eyes. Maybe it was just the depth of her shock at finding her sister dead in the same room and in the same manner as her mother. But she'd been too evasive about Sarah's *information.*

She wasn't telling him everything.

"You were the first one to find her, right?"

Anna nodded, looking at her fingertips.

"Don't worry, your fingers won't turn black, but you might want to wash the sticky residue off once we're done here." He paused, watching her. Most people, especially people with something to hide, couldn't stand to let the silence stretch for more than a few seconds.

While he waited, he compared her to her sister and her mother. A wave of disgust hit him when he thought of Lou Ann Wallace. She'd been married to Leland Hendricks, but she'd ended up as a notch on Jim McKinney's belt. She'd been just one of the women his lothario father had wooed and won. He'd never been indiscreet, but in a small town, there were no secrets.

From what he'd seen, Sarah hadn't changed since high school. Her hair was a garish shade of blond with dark roots. Her makeup had been applied with a heavy hand. And her tight skirt and revealing blouse made her the spitting image of her mother.

How had Anna turned out so differently? It didn't matter, he told himself. She was still Lou Ann's daughter. And because of that, he had a built-in aversion to her.

She moistened her lips and looked up at him. "When I came in downstairs, the desk clerk gave me a key and pointed the way to the room. The door was locked. So I knocked, but when she didn't answer, I used the key and went on in."

Anna's green eyes turned dark. "She was just lying there—on the floor. Her face was—" she cleared her throat "—discolored. Her hair was matted on the right—no, the left side of her head, and there was blood on the floor."

"The door was locked?"

As she nodded, Zane took her hands in his and looked at the palms, then turned them over and examined the backs. "Did you touch her?"

"No. I rushed over and knelt down. I was going to—" she paused for a second, looking confused "—take her hand, check for a pulse. I'm not sure what I was going to do. But her eyes were so dull. I knew she was dead."

"Annie?" Zane tightened his grip on her hands and bent his head to meet her gaze. "Are you absolutely certain she was dead when you got here?"

She nodded, her eyes glistening with tears.

"How? If you didn't touch her."

"I'm a journalist. I've covered homicides, suicides, accidents." Her shoulders tightened visibly. "I've seen my share of death. It's in the eyes."

She was right about that. "What time did you get here?"

"It was seven thirty-three when I knocked on the door. I looked at my watch and thought about how late I was."

"Good. That'll help pinpoint the time of death. Now did you see anyone? Anyone at all?"

"No one but the desk clerk."

"What about him? What did he say? Did he indicate that anyone else had been around asking about your sister?"

"No. He was fiddling with his audio player. He hardly even acknowledged me. I suppose anyone could have asked for the key—" She stopped. "Is that what happened?" Her eyes widened and her generous lips parted in a little *O*.

Zane forced himself to take his eyes off her generous mouth. He looked her up and down, cataloging her, assessing her. It appeared that she worked hard at not drawing attention to herself. Her careless hair, the lack of makeup and the plain clothes ought to make her as mousy and unnoticeable as she'd been back in school. Yet somehow, they all pulled together into a fascinating whole.

It was probably just the anomaly. She was the polar opposite of her sister and mother. At least in appearance.

He watched her face as he asked his next question. "Did you move anything? Touch anything? *Take* anything?"

"No." She pulled her hands out of his grasp and rubbed her fingers together.

Her answer was too quick. She was lying. "Are you sure? We'll know from the fingerprints."

She raised her gaze to his. "I'm sure. I touched the doorknob. That's all. I may have put my hand on the wall or the table to steady myself when I first saw her."

"Okay. Then what did you do?" He retrieved swabs from the kit and swabbed her palms. It was just a precaution. But if she had touched the body, had gotten blood on her hands, even if she'd washed them, it would show up.

"Like I told you, I knelt down beside her, but it was obvious from her face and her eyes that she was dead."

She clasped her hands together in her lap and Zane saw her shoulders relax slightly. Her color was getting better, too. She was beginning to recover from the initial shock.

"So I called 9-1-1."

"On the room phone?"

"Yes." Her eyes widened. "I touched the desk and the phone. How did I forget that?"

"It's not unusual. You were in shock. What else did you touch?"

Her gaze flickered. "I don't think I touched anything else."

"What did you do while you waited for the sheriff?"

She looked away. She was about to lie— or at the very least leave something out.

"I opened the door to the hall and sat down on the chair to wait."

"You didn't see or hear anything?"

"Not until the deputy came running in. Then all of a sudden the room was full of people."

*Yeah.* And his crime scene was thoroughly contaminated.

"When did your stepfather arrive?"

"My—" For an instant she looked confused. "Leland? I guess he and the mayor got there about the same time, right behind the doctor."

"What's the problem between you and Leland Hendricks?"

Her eyes widened. "There's no problem. It's just—I don't think of him as my stepfather."

"You were pretty young when your mother married him."

"Is this pertinent?"

Zane gazed at her evenly until she blinked and looked back at her hands.

"I was fifteen. We'd been here about a year when my mother was killed."

"So you were sixteen when your sister left you with Leland Hendricks and went to Vegas."

"I lived in his house until I graduated from high school. He was essentially bankrupt, but he took care of my portion of my mother's life insurance for me, and gave it to me when I graduated."

"Who took out the policy?"

She looked puzzled. "I guess Leland did. I doubt my mother would put out that kind of money for insurance."

"What kind of money? How much did the policy pay?"

"Sarah and I each got a hundred thousand. I don't know what Leland got."

Zane made a note to check on the insurance. By rights, it should have been hard as hell for Leland to get his portion of the insurance. As the husband of the murdered woman, he'd have been investigated thoroughly by the insurance company before they released the first dime.

"What did you do after you graduated from

high school? Did you spend summers with Leland?"

She lowered her gaze to her hands. "I went to college in Dallas. Once I moved, we didn't keep in touch."

*She was alone.* The compassion that had lurked just under the surface ever since he'd seen her sitting staring at her sister's body rose again. She'd lost her mother and her sister when she was sixteen. Zane felt another layer of respect and admiration for her.

"So Leland was never like a father to you."

She smiled wryly. "No. He was more like a business manager. But in his defense, his wife had been murdered and his little boy had disappeared."

"Justin. Donna's child."

She nodded. "Poor Justin. He was so cute, but he was like a little pawn, being pulled back and forth between Donna and Leland."

"Then there was Joey."

"At least Joey was old enough to think for herself. She was a couple of years younger than me. We never got to be friends, but from what I saw, Joey hated everybody—Donna, Leland and Lou Ann. Especially Donna. She told me once that she suspected her mother of hiding Justin away, just to keep him from Leland."

"Could that have been true?"

Anna rubbed her eyes and pushed her hair back wearily. "I don't think so. I remember Donna screaming that my mother had stolen Justin. But back then Donna was a lush and a druggie. She barely made sense most of the time."

"Do you think your mother stole the boy?"

Anna's clear green eyes met Zane's. She shrugged. "I don't know. Mom couldn't stand little kids. She used to beg Leland to give custody back to Donna. She said she was too old to have a screaming kid around."

She paused, and her green eyes turned sharp as a shard of glass. "Do you think your father killed my mother?"

Zane steeled himself not to show any reaction to her question. "I don't 'think' anybody did. My job is to find the facts."

He glanced at his watch. Anna had given him a lot to think about. He was more and more convinced that Sarah Wallace's murder was connected to Lou Ann's death sixteen years ago.

But right now he needed to get back downstairs. He quickly finished labeling the swabs and loaded everything back into the case and stood.

"I need your clothes."

She tensed. "My clothes? Why?" She waved a hand. "Never mind. I know. You'll either eliminate my fingerprints and any trace evidence on my clothes or you'll use it to prove I touched her. I'd tell you it's a waste of time and effort, but you won't believe me and I'll just end up more frustrated. I assume I can have something to change into?"

Zane suppressed a smile at her frosty words. She was definitely over the worst of the shock of finding her sister. He was glad. She'd been positively green around the gills. He didn't need a fainting key witness. He had too many loose ends already.

He decided not to remind her that there was a third possibility for use of trace evidence from her clothes. Not that he believed for a moment that she'd killed her sister, but the presence or absence of any evidence that Anna had touched Sarah's body could tie up at least one of his loose ends.

"Did you bring a bag?"

"Just an overnighter. It's still in my car."

"Is the door unlocked?"

"Yes. I parked in front of the inn. I didn't

expect to be here long." Her face threatened to crumple and her eyes welled with tears.

Zane turned away, giving her the illusion of privacy, and pulled out his cell phone. He pressed the front desk's number. "Bring up Ms. Wallace's bag. It's in her car, right out front."

He pocketed his phone and angled his head at her as she wiped the dampness from her cheeks. "I thought you and your sister weren't close."

Anna shot him a withering look. "So I shouldn't be upset that she's dead?" Her voice cracked just a bit on the word "dead."

He kept his expression carefully bland.

"She was my sister, my family. The last of my family. And family means a lot to me."

*Family.* A splinter of regret lodged under his breastbone. Family meant a lot to him, too—or it had once. Up until sixteen years ago. Until the night his father, who'd never been able to keep it in his pants, had killed Lou Ann.

It didn't matter that Jim McKinney had beaten the rap because of a technicality. He'd succeeded in destroying his own life and the lives of his wife and sons. Zane hated him for that.

"What about your dad?"

Anna's jaw muscles twisted. "We don't know who he is. Mom would never tell us."

Zane heard the creaky elevator doors, then footsteps approaching. He opened the door. The desk clerk stepped a few inches into the room and held out a pilot's bag.

Zane took it and leveled a look at him. "Did you get me that master key?"

"Ain't but one."

"One's enough for me."

The clerk shuffled, his too long jeans swishing on the burnished hardwood floors. "Mr. Matheson left me in charge."

Zane didn't even bother answering, he just held out his hand. After more shuffling, the clerk took a large key out of his pocket and handed it over.

"What time do you get off work?" Zane asked as he slipped the key onto his key ring.

"Why?"

Zane narrowed his gaze.

"Midnight."

"Don't go anywhere. I need you to make a statement."

"But I was—" He stopped. "No problem." He stuck one hand in his pocket and eyed Anna, but didn't move. He obviously expected a tip.

Zane took a step toward him. "Get back to the desk," he said, and slammed the door.

He set the bag on the bed. "Open it."

"I guess you're just in the habit of ordering everyone around," Anna said shortly as she got up and unzipped the bag.

"It's one of the perks of my job. I assume you don't mind if I have a look inside."

"Do I have a choice?"

"You've already opened it voluntarily."

She shrugged.

He quickly went through the contents, ticking off each item as he removed it. A pair of slip-on tennis shoes. Pants. A blouse. A little tank top with skinny shoulder straps.

Then his fingers touched something soft and silky—panties. He swallowed. They were tiny bikinis, several pair in a rainbow of colors, including a sort of beige he had a feeling would blend perfectly with Anna's skin.

There was an unopened package of stockings and a small makeup bag. He checked the zippered compartment. A miniature digital camera, a pocketknife and a key-ring-size can of pepper spray were tucked between a hand mirror and a clear plastic bag containing a toothbrush and toothpaste.

"I thought you didn't decide to come until the last minute?" He looked at her from under his brows. "It looks to me like you put a lot of thought into packing this case."

"I keep it in my car. I'm an investigative journalist. Sometimes I have last-minute, out-of-town assignments."

He put everything back into her bag and zipped it closed. Stepping over to the closet he retrieved the plastic bag the inn provided for laundry and handed it to her. "I need everything you have on," he said.

Her gaze snapped to his and she swallowed. "Everything?"

He nodded, clenching his jaw. *Everything.* Zane didn't like the way his body went on immediate sexual alert.

"Can I—may I take a shower?"

*Whoa, boy.* The image that slammed into his brain when she'd said *shower* surprised and stirred him.

He didn't know what the hell was wrong with him tonight. In all the years he'd been a Ranger, he'd never imagined a victim or a witness naked. Naked and wet, with rivulets of water running between her small perfect breasts and over her flat tummy.

He clenched his jaw and gave himself a mental shake. Anna was a witness. His most important witness, because she'd found Sarah's body.

He forced himself to consider her question with his usual focused objectivity. He was sure she hadn't lied about touching her sister's body. But she *was* lying about something. He could sense it. He could almost see it. She wasn't comfortable with lying and it showed.

He had her fingerprints. Once the crime scene was processed, he could approximate how long she'd been in the room and what, if anything, she'd done before she called the sheriff. He could get a hair sample at any time and skin tags from her clothing.

He shrugged, keeping his eyes averted. "Sure. Go ahead. But hand me your clothes first. I need to get back to my crime scene."

A strand of hair that had slipped out of her barrette lay across her forehead. She pushed it back with a shaky hand and met his gaze. "Thank you."

He hadn't seen her cry, but he hadn't missed the deep sadness and horror in her green eyes. A flash of insight told him she was about to lose her grip on her emotions. She'd probably cry as soon as she stepped into the shower.

"Put everything in that plastic bag. *Everything.*"

Her cheeks turned pink as she went into the bathroom and closed the door.

The bathroom was tiny. Anna set her overnight bag on the toilet seat and opened it. It was disconcerting that Zane had touched her things. She looked at her bikini panties. *All her things.*

Now he wanted every stitch she had on to process for evidence. She wondered if he was just torturing her. What possible need could he have for her underwear? What if she hadn't had a change of clothes in her car? What would he have done?

The answer to that question hit her like a freight train. Her pulse raced and she cursed under her breath.

If she'd been thinking clearly, she could have pretended she didn't have any clothes. Maybe he'd have brought her Sarah's suitcase.

"Come on, Anna. Zane McKinney is no fool. The suitcase is evidence. Think like an investigator," she muttered as she slipped off her tailored gray slacks and unbuttoned her blouse.

A discreet but insistent knock sounded at the door. "Hurry up. Hand your clothes out and I'll leave you to take your shower."

She slipped out of her panties and bra and dropped them into the bag on top of her shirt and pants and shoes, then thought better of it and pushed them down to the bottom of the bag. She couldn't bear thinking of him touching her intimate things—the things she'd worn all day. It was excruciatingly embarrassing, and yet at the same time it sent a perverse little thrill through her.

She could only hope it was as unsettling for him as it was for her. So far, his commanding presence had made her feel as awkward and self-conscious as she'd been back in high school.

With shaky hands she wrapped a towel around her body and tucked the corner in to secure it. Then she opened the bathroom door a crack and tossed the bag out onto the floor.

"There. I hope you enjoy pawing through my clothes."

"I don't paw. Thank you. I'll lock the door on my way out."

She listened intently until she heard him press the lock and shut the door.

He was gone. *Finally.* She was alone. Relief made her eyes sting and her throat close up. From the moment she'd found Sarah's body, she'd been clinging to control like a drowning man clutching a life preserver. But now nobody was watching. A sob erupted from her chest.

*No.* She clenched her fists. She would *not* break down. The last thing she needed was to be crippled by emotion.

She turned on the shower and adjusted the water temperature. But before she stepped into the tub, she reached over and locked the bathroom door, not really sure why, except that it made her feel better.

She stepped under the hot, peppering spray. And as the refreshing water washed the clinging odor of death from her nostrils, she finally gave in and cried for her sister.

ZANE HEADED BACK to Room One. As he approached the yellow crime scene tape, he saw a stranger standing next to Jon Evans. The doctor was peeling off his exam gloves and talking to the stocky middle-aged man.

Jon glanced up as Zane stalked toward them.

"Zane. This is Deputy Brian Enis. He went with Carley to the hospital."

Zane eyed the man. He looked familiar. "Deputy. You should have sent someone to the hospital with the sheriff. Your primary job was to secure the two crime scenes."

Enis's face turned brick red. He tugged on his belt. "Well, McKinney, I reckon it's a good thing you're here. You can handle everything yourself, just like you did back in high school."

*Enis*. Zane remembered now. Brian Enis's younger brother Billy had been second-string quarterback Zane's senior year. He'd only played in one game. Obviously, Enis still resented Zane for outshining his brother. He'd just have to get in line.

"Are we going to have a problem here, Enis?"

The deputy smirked. "Nope. I'll be tickled pink to prove your daddy killed Sarah Wallace just like he offed Lou Ann."

Anger sent blood roaring through Zane's ears. It took all his self-control not to deck the man. The hell of it was, he needed him. Until he had time to think about putting together a Ranger task force, he had to rely on local law enforcement.

He leveled a gaze at the smirking deputy and watched in satisfaction as sweat popped out on the man's florid temples. "Anyone working with me needs to be unbiased. Do I need to ask for your badge, *Deputy?*"

Enis swallowed and puffed out his chest. "You can't. I'm in charge when Carley's not here."

"Not this time. I'm the lead investigator on this case and that means I'm in charge of this town. If you can't—or won't—work with me, I'll make sure the mayor and the governor both know that."

Enis dropped his gaze to his shoes.

"I guess we understand each other. Now take this kit and process the room. It's contaminated, so it's going to be difficult. Be sure to preserve all of Ms. Wallace's belongings, and catalog everything. I want your full report and every bit of the evidence at the police station by 7:00 a.m."

"But it's nearly midnight."

"Then that gives you seven hours, doesn't it?"

The deputy fumed but he didn't say anything, just stomped out of the room.

Zane spoke briefly with Dr. Evans but the doctor didn't have any further information.

"I'll have my report for you by seven," Evans said with a smile.

"Thanks, Jon. What about the body?"

"I've called for an ambulance to transport her to County General. How do you want to handle the postmortem?"

"I'll call Dallas and have them contact you."

Zane walked downstairs with Jon, only to find the lobby filling up again with curious people. He stalked over to the desk.

"I told you to keep everybody out."

The surly desk clerk shuffled his feet and pulled the ear bud microphones out of his ears. "Ain't no way. Nobody's listening to me."

As angry as Zane was, he could see the boy's point. Still— "Did you think about locking the doors?"

"Front door don't lock. At least, I don't have a key for it."

That gave Zane pause. "Where's Bill Matheson?"

"Out of town."

Nobody had mentioned that. "Have he and his wife been notified about the murder?"

The boy shrugged. "Not my job. I just work here."

Zane turned on his heel and faced the small crowd of people who were watching him with blatant curiosity.

"All you people. Unless you have information pertinent to Sarah Wallace's death, go home. Let us do our job."

A woman decked out in a pricey pantsuit and jewelry that was too understated to be fake stepped forward. "I'm Donna Hendricks. You may not remember me—" She paused, obviously expecting him to contradict her.

Zane obliged. "Oh, yes, ma'am, I do." He

would have known her anywhere. Her bright red hair and air of superiority made the air around her crackle.

Her little boy had disappeared just a few days before Lou Ann Wallace had been murdered all those years ago. As far as he knew the child had never been found. The tragedy had made national headlines.

At the time, Zane had been away at school, and already sick and tired of Justice and everybody in it. In his opinion, the town could have been lifted right out of a particularly sleazy soap opera with Donna and Leland Hendricks as its two main stars.

They'd been married for fourteen years and divorced for two at the time of the murder, and their fights were legendary, as was Donna's substance abuse problem. Their two children, a teenage daughter and a toddler son, were pawns in their hurtful game.

After a messy divorce and an even messier court battle, Leland and his new trophy wife, Lou Ann Wallace, had gotten custody of the children.

Donna laid a perfectly manicured hand on his sleeve. "I just want you to know that Leland doesn't have an alibi for the time of the murder."

Zane's brows rose along with his level of frustration. "Ms. Hendricks, you shouldn't be here. Why don't you go on home? Someone will talk to you tomorrow."

"Don't try to dismiss me, Zane McKinney. This is important."

"Okay, then. How do you know the time of the murder?"

Donna's pale blue eyes wavered. "I heard it was some time around seven o'clock."

Zane sighed. "You heard it. From whom?"

"What difference does that make? I'm telling you, Leland could have killed her."

Zane recognized the near hysteria in her voice. He wished he had time to indulge her desperate need to discredit the man she blamed for the death of her child. It was possible she had a tidbit of information he could use, but she would have to wait.

He couldn't do everything at once, and besides, Donna Hendricks was not at the top of his list of credible witnesses.

"Ms. Hendricks, you need to go on home. I'll get someone out to interview you as soon as I can."

He faced the crowd again. "I meant it, folks. It's after midnight. Go home. Go to bed. There's nothing more to see. And you're hindering a murder investigation."

A hushed murmur rippled through the crowd, which had begun to slowly file out of the large, richly appointed lobby of the Matheson Inn. How was he going to keep nosy townspeople away from the inn? He wiped a weary hand over his face.

"Zane?"

He froze, his hand at his mouth. "Mom?"

Stella McKinney stepped in front of him. A bright pink jogging suit hung on her slight frame. On her feet were pink running shoes and her hair was stiffly sprayed into the same tight style she'd always worn.

Zane's heart squeezed in a combination of compassion and sadness. She looked so small, so beaten down. And it was all his dad's fault.

"It's been a long time, honey."

Okay, not all his dad's fault. Zane knew exactly how long it had been since he'd seen his family. It was five years ago on Christmas. He remembered as if it were yesterday.

His dad hadn't changed. Maybe his good humor had seemed forced, and his skin had looked a little big for his body. To Zane, it hadn't altered the fact that his affair with Lou Ann Wallace and the mystery surrounding her death had destroyed their family.

Every Christmas, his mother had tried to

keep up tradition for Zane and Sloan. She'd decorated the house and baked cookies, but each year her heart was less and less in it.

That year, on Christmas Eve, she'd given up and retreated to her room. Zane had left town the same day, and he'd never been back.

"I know, Mom. I've been busy." He leaned over and kissed her on the cheek. She smelled like baby powder and hair spray. The familiar scents took him back to a time when her face hadn't been etched with bitter lines and the look in her eyes wasn't resigned and distant. "What are you doing here? It's late."

Her eyes darted around the room like a bird's and her knuckles grew white. "I just wanted to see you. See how you were doing."

Guilt gnawed at Zane's gut. "You should be at home. I was going to come by."

She nodded jerkily. "Have you seen your father?"

"Yeah." So that was it. She was afraid his dad had done this. "Mom, is there something you need to tell me? Something about Dad? About tonight?"

"No. No, of course not." Her voice was shrill and edged with panic. She unclasped her fingers and folded her arms. "You look thin. You don't eat enough."

Zane smiled. Now she sounded more like

his mother. "I'm fine, Mom. I've been working out."

"Sloan says he doesn't see much of you."

"Look, Mom. I'll see you tomorrow or maybe the next day, okay? Right now I've got a lot of work to do. Let me get somebody to take you home."

"No need for that." Jim McKinney's voice boomed in Zane's ears. His father pushed past the few remaining rubberneckers to grip his wife's arm. "Come on, Stella. Let's go home."

His mother's eyes grew dark and cold as she pulled her arm free. "*Now* you want to go home?" Her voice dripped ice.

Jim tried to put his arm around her shoulders, but she ducked away. "I was worried about you," he said.

She sniffed and started for the door.

Zane watched them leave, his heart heavy. He shook his head and tried to dislodge the gnawing guilt that threatened to overtake him.

He had to focus. He had to think like a lawman—like a Ranger. And as a Ranger, he knew what he'd just heard was vitally important to his investigation.

His dad had told him earlier that he was home eating dinner at the approximate time

Sarah died. But from his mother's comment, it sounded like Jim McKinney hadn't been home all evening.

Zane took out his PDA and made a note as a cautious formality—a habit. He shook his head at himself for even bothering to note it, because there was no way he'd ever forget his mother's telling words.

His stomach clenched.

Once again, just like sixteen years before, a murder had been committed in Justice, and his father didn't have an alibi.

## Chapter Three

Anna heard a noise. Startled, she turned off the shower and stood still, listening. She tried to place the sound—give it substance—but she couldn't. It had sounded creaky, vaguely metallic. Maybe it was the groaning of the old hot water pipes. Goodness knew she'd given them a workout.

She ran her fingers through her wet hair. All the shampoo had been rinsed out long ago, yet she'd continued to let the hot water pour over her heated skin, wishing all the while it could wash away the horrible truth and send her back to her structured, secure life. The life that had crumbled like a sand castle when her sister had called the day before.

She reached out to push the shower curtain aside and heard the sound again. It was definitely metallic—a click, like a door closing.

She froze, her breath caught in her throat. Her fingers gripped the plastic curtain.

*Calm down,* she admonished herself. She was just spooked by her sister's death. Lord knew she had a right to be. The inn had been built before the Civil War, and old buildings made noise. The walls were paper-thin. The sound had probably been a door to another room opening and closing.

Taking a deep breath, Anna pushed the curtain aside and grabbed a towel. After quickly drying off, she hurriedly slipped on her camisole and beige underwear from her overnight bag. As soon as she dried her hair she could go to bed. Although if the building kept up its odd creaking, she wouldn't sleep a wink. Not tonight.

Looking in the mirror at her shiny-clean face, she couldn't help but see the face of her dead sister. Poor Sarah was in that room downstairs alone, being pawed over by the doctor and Zane McKinney.

Tears glistened in her eyes. How could she sleep, knowing Zane wouldn't rest until he'd been over every square inch of the room where Sarah had died? Until he'd touched everything her sister had brought with her.

*Everything.* Her pulse sped up until it

hammered in her ears. If he looked hard enough, he just might find Sarah's secret.

And that couldn't happen. Not yet. She had to go back down there. She needed to be there, to protect her sister and her sister's things.

She squeezed droplets of water out of her hair with one hand as she searched in the overnight bag for her hairbrush. Of course it wasn't there. It was in her purse, which she'd left on the bed.

She opened the bathroom door and stepped out into the bedroom, shivering when cool air hit her damp skin. Her purse was on the far side of the bed. She propped a knee on the mattress and reached for it.

All at once the door swung open.

Anna shrieked, lost her footing and sprawled across the bed.

Zane McKinney halted in the doorway, shock and irritation darkening his already grim expression. His gaze swept her from head to toe and a flicker of something hot flared in his blue-gray eyes. Then his brows drew down and his jaw clenched.

"Why is this door unlocked?"

"How did you get in here?" Anna asked at the same time. She scrambled awkwardly to her feet, hyperaware of her state of undress. She tugged at the bedspread, hoping to use it to wrap around her, but it was tightly tucked in.

So she crossed her arms and glared at him. "You didn't lock the door."

"I did lock it."

"I think it's obvious that you didn't."

He examined the old door with its age-darkened hardware, then looked back at her. His steely gaze burned like a laser as it slowly moved down her body and back up again. When he met her gaze his eyes were smoky. And Anna could have sworn that for an instant, lust gleamed in their blue-gray depths.

Her knees grew weak and her mouth went dry. She was practically naked, standing in front of the best-looking man Justice, Texas, had ever produced. Mortification piled on top of her other emotions—fear, grief, shock and a totally inappropriate attraction to Zane McKinney.

"Have you been in the bathroom all this time?" he barked, frowning.

She bristled at his sharp tone. "Yes. Why? Are you afraid I used all the hot water?"

His mouth thinned in disapproval. "This is serious business, Annie. I locked the door. Did you unlock it?"

"I told you no. I did not unlock the door."

"Then what happened?"

She propped her fists on her hips. "You're asking me? You're the one who made the mistake. And trust me, I'm not thrilled to find out I took a shower in an unlocked room."

"Did you hear anything?"

"Like what?" she snapped. Then she remembered the creaking and the click, and a shudder racked her body. "Wait. I did, but I thought it was the pipes."

"When?"

"I'm sure it was the pipes."

"Annie!" His voice rose in frustration.

"Just a few minutes ago. I thought I heard a creaking noise, so I turned off the water. Then I heard it again. It sounded like a door closing—or opening." She shrugged. "Maybe."

Her stomach turned over. "Are you thinking someone tried to get in here?"

Zane nodded grimly. "I'm thinking someone did get in. I'll have Enis dust for prints."

"But why would anyone—"

She stopped as he walked over to her, close enough that she had to look up to meet his gaze. Close enough that if he hadn't stopped when he did, his summer-weight jacket would have brushed the tips of her barely covered breasts. He smelled of soap and leather. Like a man. Whatever cologne he used was subtle and expensive.

"Annie, what are you not telling me?"

She stepped backward and her legs hit the bedside table. "Nothing. I just walked out of the bathroom."

"Not about that. About your sister. You're holding something back."

"No, I'm not." Anna slid sideways, away from his commanding presence. She was covered only by a few scraps of nylon. She felt exposed, vulnerable, and although she'd never admit it to him, it spooked the hell out of her that someone might have sneaked into her room while she was in the shower.

"Yes, you are. You're not a very good liar. It's a wonder you can make a living as a reporter."

"I'm a *journalist.* And I am not lying."

He shrugged. "Fine then. Get some clothes on."

Her face burned at his arched tone. "What a great idea. I plan to. And as soon as I dry my hair I'm going to bed."

"No. You're coming with me. I need you to write out and sign your statement."

Anna stared at him in disgust. "On the cases I've covered, the strong-arm tactics were reserved for suspects. Surely you don't—" She stopped and narrowed her eyes at him. "You do! You consider me a suspect, don't you?"

He didn't answer.

"Look, Zane. I didn't kill my sister. I don't see why my written statement can't wait until morning. You already know everything I know."

His mouth quirked in a wry smile, the famous smile that had won the hearts of all the high school girls and made the other guys jealous. Anna had never been on the receiving end of it before. It was lethally sexy.

"See? There you go lying again. But don't worry, Annie." His smile stayed in place but his eyes turned cold and hard. "Before I'm done, I'll know everything you know. Including what your sister told you."

"I have no idea what you're talking about," Anna said haughtily. "Please lock the door on your way out. And stop calling me Annie!"

She turned and fled into the bathroom. Slamming the door, she leaned against it, biting her lip in consternation. He was good. In the few years she'd worked as an investigative journalist, she'd seen her share of lawmen. They ranged from dense as a fence post to brilliant, from haphazard and sloppy to obsessively meticulous. But she'd never met anyone like Zane.

His changeable eyes had burned like laser beams, probing past her defenses. She had no doubt he meant every word he said. He wouldn't stop until he knew everything about the murder.

*Oh, brother.* This was going to be harder than she'd thought.

THE NEXT MORNING as Zane stepped off the elevator on the fourth floor trauma ward at County General Hospital, he heard Carley. Her voice echoed off the pale green walls.

"You can't keep me here without my consent!"

Zane headed toward the source of the sound. When he stepped into the hospital room, he found Sheriff Carley Matheson grimacing as she tried to reach the ties on the back of her hospital gown. A tired-looking nurse stood beside her holding a tiny paper cup and a plastic water jug with a flexible straw.

"Hello, Carley." He grinned. "I see you haven't changed a bit since high school." She might be Sheriff of Justice, but to Zane she still looked like the little girl with braces and a bedraggled ponytail who'd followed his younger brother Sloan around like a puppy.

Her eyes widened. "Zane! I mean, Lieutenant McKinney." Her hand lifted automatically to her hair.

"From what I can see, you're doing fine. I assume you know why I'm here."

The nurse proffered the cup. Carley sent her a withering glare.

Zane almost chuckled. "Come on, Carley, be a good girl and take your medicine."

"Mind your own business—sir." She accepted the cup with ill grace. "I'm not taking any pain pills," she warned the nurse.

"We've been over this, Sheriff Matheson," the nurse said wearily. "This is an antibiotic, to keep your bullet wound from getting infected."

Carley made a face as she tipped the cup and let the tablet fall into her mouth. Then she took a huge swig of water. "There. Happy now?"

The nurse sent Zane a grateful nod as she left the room.

Carley cocked her head to one side. "I was surprised when your captain told me he was sending you."

Zane grimaced. "No more surprised than me. The way he put it, he had two choices. He could send a Ranger who knew nothing about Justice and its scandalous past and wait a week for him to get up to speed, or he could send a Ranger who knew everything that happened sixteen years ago, but who might be prejudiced."

Carley eased carefully back against the pillows, her lips thinning in an obvious effort not to wince. "I see. And you assured him you could remain totally objective."

*Objective.* Hardly.

He shook his head. "Nope. I told him I was definitely prejudiced. That as far as I'm concerned, Jim McKinney is a prime suspect, just like he was back then."

"Zane." Carley hesitated. "I want you to know I'd give anything to change what I saw that night. I know how much it hurt your family—"

He waved a hand. "You were thirteen. You saw what you saw and you told the truth. I have no illusions about my dad. He was a rounder then, and I'm sure he still is." Bitterness tasted like bile in his mouth.

Time to get back to the present. He frowned. "I need you to tell me everything you saw last night."

She nodded. "I gave Enis a statement on

the way here, but I'm afraid I was pretty much out of it."

"I've talked to him. You're right. Your account was sketchy. Start at the beginning." He took out a digital recorder and turned it on.

"Happy to, sir." She closed her eyes. "I was sitting in my office, doing paperwork. There's never enough time to get it all done. A movement out the window caught my eye. When I looked up, I saw someone running across the inn parking lot."

"What time was this?"

"My best guess—about seven-twenty. Because when I looked at my watch on the way outside a few moments later it was seven twenty-three."

"Good." Zane made a note on his PDA. "But wait a minute. Seven-twenty is working late?"

Carley nodded, amused. "This is small-town Texas, Zane. The sheriff's office closes at five. The deputies and I take turns being on call."

"Crime from nine to five." Zane shook his head. "Okay, tell me exactly what you saw."

"There was no moon. The only light came from the sconces beside the inn's back door.

All I saw was a dark figure running across the inn's parking lot."

"Male? Female?"

She closed her eyes and scrunched up her face. "He or she had on pants. Their upper body was in total shadow. All I saw were legs and shoes. Maybe cowboy boots."

Zane sighed. Her description was almost word for word from Deputy Enis's report. "So you couldn't distinguish anything identifiable? Height? Weight? Hair color?"

"No. Well, I'd say the person was not very tall. Mostly all I saw was a dark blob with legs. I pursued him, but by the time I got to the parking lot, he'd disappeared into the woods. I followed, but—" She gestured toward her side.

"You were shot."

"And I went down like a girl. If I hadn't been such a wimp, maybe I could have caught him."

"You were at a disadvantage. The shooter was concealed by darkness. You were outlined by the inn's lights. You were an easy target. You could have been killed."

"I couldn't even hang on to the bullet. It went right through. Do you know how much of a laughingstock I am now?" Her voice turned mocking. "The sheriff was stopped by a flesh wound."

"Stop feeling sorry for yourself." He softened his words with a smile. "You were lucky."

"I guess. Of course, now I'm not even in charge of my own town."

"Your job is to concentrate on getting better. I'll take care of the investigation."

"You believe the guy who shot me killed Sarah Wallace?"

"It looks that way. Jon estimated her time of death as between 7:00 p.m. and 7:30 p.m. With your information and Anna Wallace's statement, we're getting the time narrowed down to around seven-fifteen or seven-twenty."

"Luis told me Anna found the body. That must have been awful for her."

"Yeah." Zane didn't want to think about Anna right now. He tended to get distracted when he did. "Nothing else you can add?"

Carley shook her head. "I'm sorry, Zane. I wish there were."

He checked his watch. He needed to get back to Justice. He patted Carley's hand. "Take care, and don't give the nurses too hard a time. I'll see you later."

"Wait. Have you seen your parents?"

He wasn't going there. Not now. "Doesn't matter. I'm here to investigate a murder, not visit my folks. But speaking of parents, what about yours?"

"Zane, please don't tell them. They're on a summer-long camper trip—first time they've gotten away in years. If they come running back here, what's that going to say about me as sheriff?"

"That you have caring parents?"

"Please."

"Won't everybody in town call them anyway?"

Carley shifted in bed and winced, but her eyes sparkled. "Dad just got a new cell phone, and nobody but me knows his number."

Zane frowned. "I need information about the inn."

"I can tell you anything you need to know."

"I'll make you a deal. I won't call them if you'll be a good girl and do what the nurses tell you."

She stuck her tongue out at him as he turned to leave.

He paused at the door. "Oh, I almost forgot. Where are the records from Lou Ann's murder? I need to go over them."

Carley's brows knit. "Probably in the basement with all the other records, unless they were sent to the Department of Archives and History for storage." She perked up. "Hey! You think whoever killed Lou Ann killed Sarah. I've been thinking the same thing."

"I just don't want to leave any loose ends."

"You know who would know where those records are. Sloan. If he sent any to Archives while he was sheriff, he'd be able to tell you which ones."

Zane nodded and left. *Sloan.* Of course his brother would know. He'd been sheriff of Justice for five years, and he'd beaten out Carley for deputy three years prior to that.

Zane should have realized he wouldn't make it through this investigation without involving Sloan. He might have to work with his younger brother, but he didn't have to like it.

BACK IN JUSTICE, things were pretty well under control. Sarah Wallace's body had been transported to County General for autopsy. With the bumbling help of Deputy Enis, Zane had managed to finish processing Sarah's room, although it had been so thoroughly contaminated he didn't hold out much hope of gaining any useful prints or trace evidence. He told Enis to collect Sarah's belongings and lock them up in the evidence room at the police station.

Deputy Spinoza hadn't fared much better at the second crime scene, where Carley had been shot. Zane had examined the area earlier that morning, before he'd visited her. Her account matched the physical findings.

The back door to the inn opened into a small, poorly lit parking lot. Beyond that was a wooded area. To the right was the sheriff's office. Carley's office window was perfectly aligned with the back door of the inn.

Zane sat in her squeaky desk chair and cursed as he eyed the view from the window.

If there had been a full moon last night, or if the parking lot behind the inn had been appropriately lighted, Carley would have seen the face of the person who shot her.

Zane would have his killer. He had no doubt that the same person who murdered Sarah Wallace had shot Carley. And he knew in his gut they'd also killed Lou Ann sixteen years ago. The question was why.

Pulling out his cell phone, he dialed his captain. "Where are you on getting me a team out here?"

Captain Hardy sighed. "I'm working on it. You know the president is scheduled to present a commendation to the four Rangers who brought down that child-smuggling ring at the border. The governor wants a big turnout."

"Are you saying I'm not getting any help?"

"It'll be a couple of days. Can you hang in there with local law enforcement for the next thirty-six hours?"

"If I have to."

"Good. That's why I sent you."

"Thank you, sir. And thanks for getting me a transcriptionist."

"Lottie Hagan works in my office. So she's duly sworn in and knows how to handle confidential matters. She's one of the best."

"I appreciate that. One less thing I have to worry about. Keep me informed." Zane disconnected and pocketed his phone just as Lottie came in with the typed statements from the desk clerk, Leland Hendricks and Anna Wallace.

Zane thanked her and gave her Carley's tape to transcribe. Then he glanced through the statements. Deputy Luis Spinoza had taken the desk clerk's and Leland Hendricks's statement. Zane probably should have talked to Leland himself, but he was just one man. He couldn't do everything.

Leland claimed he was at home during the time of the murder. Since the murder occurred on Sunday his house staff were off duty. So, no, there was no one who could corroborate his story. Zane flipped the page. Leland had planned a quiet night at home. He'd fixed a sandwich, had a couple of beers and was watching a DVD when he got a phone call telling him about Sarah's murder.

So Leland Hendricks had no alibi. *Great.*

Zane kept reading. Spinoza asked Leland if he'd spoken to Sarah. Leland's answer was no, but Spinoza had placed a sticky note in the margin. *Delay in answering. Check phone records for incoming calls.*

A tiny seed of excitement began to grow in Zane's chest. Spinoza was a good lawman. If Leland was lying and Sarah had called him, what else was he lying about? And who else had Sarah called?

He reached for his cell phone and called the deputy sheriff. "Spinoza, McKinney here. I'm reading Leland Hendricks's statement. You think Sarah called him?"

"I don't know, but he definitely hesitated before answering."

"Have we checked the hotel records for outgoing and incoming calls?"

"Yes, sir. None from Room One."

"And we didn't find a cell phone on her."

"No, sir. But there was a receipt in her purse for one of those prepaid phones. If she brought it with her, somebody took it."

"Thanks, Spinoza. Good job. Follow up on that receipt. Find out what the number was and see if you can match it to any resident's calls."

"You want me to check everybody in town?"

"Get Burns to help you. Start with those whose statements we've gotten." Zane disconnected and set Leland's statement aside.

The other two statements were from Richie Blackwell, the desk clerk, and Anna. Predictably, Richie had no information. Zane muttered a few choice curse words as he skimmed the one-word answers that were all Spinoza had managed to extract from the kid. Nothing there.

So far, if he were to believe the statements, Leland and Richie were clueless about what happened that night. But Zane wasn't taking any of the statements at face value. He picked up Anna Wallace's statement. Certainly not hers. He turned to the last page and looked at her small neat signature.

His brain fed him a vision of her standing in the middle of her room in nothing but that tiny top and those bikini panties. He stirred uncomfortably, and cursed under his breath.

"Come on, McKinney. You're beginning to take after your old man." The idea that he might be physically attracted to the daughter of the woman who'd destroyed his family nauseated him.

His reaction to her surprised him. Not only was she the enemy, she wasn't his type. He preferred leggy blondes. Long and cool, and not interested in forever.

Still, he couldn't get Anna's slender waist, barely exposed belly button and shapely legs out of his head.

*Ah, hell.* Thinking of her reminded him he hadn't sent anyone to check for prints in her room. He was determined to find out who had sneaked into her room, because it was a cinch they were involved in Sarah's death.

He looked at his watch. It was close to noon.

He buckled on his holster, pinned his badge to his shirt and left his jacket on the rack. It wouldn't hurt to let the people of Justice see his credentials.

As he stepped out the door of the sheriff's office, he noted that there were quite a few people out and about—probably gossiping about the murder.

He walked down the wooden steps and headed toward the inn a few dozen feet away. All eyes were on him. His back stiffened.

He flexed his shoulders and consciously relaxed them, not an easy task in this town where he'd always done his best. But excelling wasn't a desirable trait in Justice. It was the opposite of fitting in.

Sloan now—Sloan had fit in. His brother had never felt the need to be the best, at least not that Zane could tell. Sloan's attitude was laid-back and confident. He genuinely liked the people in Justice and they liked him.

Zane spotted Mable Green, who was sweeping the sidewalk in front of Mable's Beau-Tique. He lifted a hand.

She stared at him a moment then hurried inside. With a wry smile, he suppressed the urge to shrug and stalked up the steps to the double glass doors of the Matheson Inn.

As he headed for the stairs, he glanced down the hall toward Room One. The garish yellow tape across the door appeared intact, but a warning tickle in his brain caused him to pause. He'd better check to be sure no one had disturbed anything.

He walked quietly toward the open door. When he glanced inside, he saw a shadowy movement. His pulse hammered. Someone was in there.

He ducked under the yellow tape and approached the figure standing in the middle of the room. It was Anna. She was pointing a camera at the dark bloodstain on the hardwood floor.

Anger burned like acid in his gut. He reached out and grabbed the camera.

Anna shrieked and whirled, propelling her elbow into Zane's midsection. Only lightning-fast reflexes kept him from having the breath knocked out of him.

"You!"

"Yep. Me. What the hell are you doing here, *Annie?* This is a crime scene."

She pinned him with her olive-green gaze. "The scene of my sister's murder. My *mother's* murder. I have a right to be here. Now give me my camera back."

"Not on your life." He pressed review on the back of the camera and quickly ran through the photos stored inside. Most were of the room where they now stood. A few earlier ones were of a local Dallas celebrity.

Anna made a halfhearted grab for it but he held it just out of her reach.

"What are you planning to do with these?" He couldn't imagine. He knew she wouldn't sell them to a newspaper or a tabloid. At least, he didn't think she would. That seemed more like something Sarah or Lou Ann might do. And somehow, each time he looked at Anna, the fact that she was related to those women fled his mind.

Her gaze flickered away from his. She tried to cover her discomfort by glancing around but he knew she was about to feed him another line.

"I wanted to study them, to see if there might be something I'd notice that you wouldn't." She gave a half shrug. "Since she was my sister." Meeting his gaze, she held out her hand. "May I please have my camera back?"

"I don't have enough manpower to assign someone to watch you. I need your assurance that you won't do this again."

Anna had known that was coming, but she wasn't ready to give in just yet. "Look at the crime scene? Why shouldn't I?" she shot back.

He crossed his arms and looked down his nearly perfect nose at her. It was obvious he wasn't going to budge until she promised. "I thought you were a *journalist*. You should know better than to disturb an active crime scene. We're not finished processing it yet."

She tried another tack. "Do you think the same person who killed my mother killed Sarah?"

The arch of his right brow told her she hadn't fooled him with the change of subject.

"I don't know. I think it's very likely, especially given what Sarah told you."

Anna's chest tightened. "What Sarah told me?"

He didn't try to hide his irritation. "I've had enough of your evasive answers. There's only one reason Sarah Wallace would have come back to Justice. And I'm betting there's only one reason you would've agreed to meet her here."

Anna composed her features as best she could and sent him a quizzical look. "What reason?"

"I'm guessing Sarah came back here with information about your mother's murder. I don't know why. Maybe she was planning to blackmail someone, or was acting out of some notion of setting the record straight."

"Blackmail?" Anna was surprised by how much his accusation hurt. "You don't think much of my family, do you?"

His blue-gray eyes turned stormy. "Do you blame me?"

She took a couple of steps toward him and

glared up into his eyes, doing her best to ignore his provocative scent. "Obviously you can't be objective, not when your father is the prime suspect in both murders. And now, you're blaming the victim for her own murder?"

"No. I'm merely being objective. I have to consider all possible motives, all likely suspects. If Sarah came to town to blackmail someone, that would go a long way toward explaining why she was killed."

They faced each other down until Anna blinked. "Okay. You say you can be objective. Even about your father?"

She saw the flicker of pain that crossed his face before he caught himself. "Especially about my father. Any illusions I might have had regarding his integrity are long gone."

Anna knew Zane hadn't meant to say so much, because as soon as the words came out of his mouth, he took a step backward and eyed the camera with too much interest.

"I asked you a question, Annie. I'm still waiting for an answer."

"You didn't ask me a question. You made an assumption."

"Fine. Here's a question. What did Sarah tell you that made you come back to Justice?

I have a feeling this is the last place you'd ever go of your own accord."

Anna swallowed. "I don't know what you're talking about. When I got here Sarah was already dead."

"What about the night before, when she called you?"

"She didn't give me any specifics. How many times do I have to tell you that?" She glanced around. "Where's that Gideon's Bible you always find in these places? Want me to swear on it?"

His lips tightened into a flat line, and he shook his head. "I need to dust for prints in your room. I hope you haven't touched the doorknobs."

"I've done my best to avoid them."

"Good." Zane turned on his heel and ducked under the crime scene tape.

"Wait," she said. "You'll need my key."

"Actually I have a master key, but I'll let you unlock the door for me. I won't barge in again." His voice held a tinge of amusement and his eyes turned the same smoky gray they had last night.

Remembering how his gaze had traveled across her skin from her head to her toes sent a liquid heat through her loins. She took a deep breath. *Focus.* Zane McKinney was all business. Anything else was only her imagination.

That was fine with her. She didn't have time for any entanglements, even if he was interested in her, which, judging from his attitude about her family, he wasn't.

"Zane. My camera."

He turned it off and handed it to her.

At the door to her room Zane stepped back and gestured for her to unlock it.

She slipped her key into the lock and turned it. Then she turned it again. And frowned. "I don't understand. It feels like—"

"Like it was already unlocked?" Zane's whispered words warmed her ear and the side of her neck. "Are you sure you locked it?"

"After last night? You'd better believe I'm sure. Don't tell me—"

He held up a hand. "Shh. Stand back."

"No. It's my room."

He scowled at her. "Go stand by the staircase. If anything happens run downstairs and call Deputy Enis."

Anna obeyed—sort of. She stood by the staircase, but as soon as Zane's back was turned, she moved a few paces toward him.

He sent an unmistakable warning glare in her direction, then pulled his weapon and held it at the ready as he pushed the door open and angled into the room.

Anna eyed his gun. It was a big one. Swallowing her fear, she took a few steps forward, until she could see in.

Her heart lodged in her throat. "Oh, no!" she squeaked.

The room had been trashed. Drawers were upside down on the floor. The mattress was half off the bed. Her bag had been emptied and the lining had been ripped out of it.

Zane checked the bathroom and the closet, then lowered his gun and faced her. "Well?"

Anna's heart clogged her throat. She gulped in air, unable to take her eyes off the destruction in the tiny room. "Well, what?"

"Now are you going to tell me the truth?"

She swallowed. "I've already told you the truth."

Zane grabbed her arm and pulled her over to where her ruined bag sat upended on the floor.

"This is not some debutante ball or high society embezzlement case, Annie. It's murder. Whoever broke in here was looking for something specific. Did they find it?"

She shook her head. No, they hadn't found it, because she hadn't been able to get her hands on it yet.

Zane turned her to face him. "The person who trashed your room and I have something in common."

Her mouth went dry as she lifted her gaze to his.

"We both know that Sarah had information that would incriminate them in your mother's murder. She was killed for it. But the killer hasn't found that something yet. You know that, too, don't you?"

She tried to shake her head but Zane's eyes held her mesmerized.

"Don't you?" he snapped. "The killer didn't find the incriminating evidence because you have it. Turn it over to me or you're going to end up the killer's next victim."

## Chapter Four

Anna swallowed hard. "I don't know what they're looking for."

Zane's blue-gray eyes assessed her. "Okay. For argument's sake, let's say that's true—"

"For *argument's* sake? You're calling me a liar?"

"No, Annie. I'm just trying to get at the truth. You say you don't know what your mysterious burglar was looking for. Can you tell me what *you* were looking for in Sarah's room?"

"I wasn't looking for anything in particular. I just wanted to see the room and get some pictures. I barely saw anything last night. I was too shocked, and then all the people came."

She thought she detected a slight softening of his expression. *Good.* Maybe he finally believed her. For the first time since they'd met, he was viewing her without skepticism, and she needed to use that to her advantage.

She looked around her trashed room. Everything she'd brought with her except her purse and her camera had been rifled. She had nothing but the clothes on her back.

"Can you tell if anything is missing?"

"I didn't bring that much, and I have my camera and my purse." She studied the mess with a journalist's eye for detail. "I don't think so."

Pausing, she sent Zane a sidelong glance. "When can I get my sister's things? I could... I could borrow some of her clothes."

His soft expression hardened. "Her suitcase, her purse and all her clothes are evidence."

Anna lowered her gaze when Zane mentioned Sarah's suitcase. She didn't want her expressive face to give her away. And she'd already tried out her "concerned journalist" look on him. He was too smart—or too suspicious—to be fooled by a sympathetic smile and stock phrases.

"And now," he continued, "so is all of your stuff. You'll just have to buy some things, or I could send someone by your apartment in Dallas."

"No." No way was anyone going to go pawing through the rest of her clothes. "So, I guess this means I won't be leaving town any time soon."

"That's right. You're my key witness. I need to keep you close."

His low, compelling voice sent her imagination soaring as she considered all the possible implications of the word close.

But she stiffened her back and stopped her wayward thoughts. He was *not* the most attractive man she'd ever seen, and he was *not* sexy. He was the enemy. He had a very big stake in the outcome of this investigation. His father's guilt or innocence.

"Fine, then. I'll make do."

He sent her an ironic smile. "At a discount supercenter?"

Her chin shot up. "If I have to."

ZANE SECURED another room for Anna. He had to process her room as yet another crime scene. Unfortunately the inn was relatively full. The only room still vacant on the second level was next door to his. In a way he was glad. He could keep an eye on her.

But in another way, one thin wall away was too close for comfort. His comment about the discount store had been a desperate attempt to catalog her with her sister and mother. But it hadn't worked.

"Here's my cell phone number," he said as she looked around the room. She dug her phone out of her purse and keyed in his number.

"Thanks." She gave him hers.

"I've got an interview back at the police station. You stay put and keep your door locked." As soon as he said it he saw that it was a waste of breath.

"I can't stay in here. As you pointed out, I need to go shopping."

"Not by yourself."

She propped her fists on her hips. "Who do you suggest I get to go with me? How about you?" Her green eyes sparked as she challenged him.

He grimaced. "If I have to."

She grinned at him as he turned to leave. "Wait a minute. Who are you interviewing?"

Zane stopped at the door. "Jim McKinney."

"Your father? I want to be there."

"No. Absolutely not."

"Listen to me, Zane McKinney. I've lost my entire family. I have to know what happened. Are you afraid to let me hear what you and Jim talk about?"

"If you knew me you wouldn't ask that

question. I'm a Texas Ranger. The fact that one of the suspects happens to be my father is irrelevant. I'll do my job."

"Good. Then you won't mind if I'm there."

"I said no."

"I'm a journalist. I've been invited in on interrogations before. I'm no novice at this. If *you* knew *me,* you'd know that I'm one of the most trusted journalists in Dallas."

He did know that. He'd requested a background check on her via e-mail first thing this morning. The response had come back almost immediately, and was filled with praise and accolades. No black marks on her career.

"Nevertheless—"

"How about this. You ask your father if it's okay. If he doesn't want me there, then I'll wait to see the transcript."

"What about the small fact that *I* don't want you there?"

"If you don't let me sit in, I'll have to assume you intend to talk to your father about something you don't want me to hear."

"Fine, we'll ask him." Zane already knew what his father would say. Jim McKinney had never in his life refused an opportunity to be with a beautiful woman.

He called Deputy Spinoza. "Luis, I've got another crime scene. Yeah. Anna Wallace's room has been turned upside down. Get over here and secure it. See if you can lift any new prints although it's probably a long shot. If the killer did it, we already know he wears gloves."

After shooting a glare in Anna's direction, he turned on his booted heel and headed back to the station. If she wanted to be in on his father's interview, she'd just have to keep up.

She did.

Anna was glad she had on running shoes, because in heels she'd have been left eating Zane's dust. Although she had a great view of his long muscular legs and trim, sexy backside. Definitely eye-candy.

Setting her jaw, she shifted her gaze to the sidewalk. By the time she stepped through the front door of the police station Jim was already there, talking with the transcriptionist. He said something to her that made her giggle, then he straightened, looking first at his son and then at her.

"Anna, how're you doing?"

She took a breath to answer, but Zane cut her off.

"She's fine. I don't have a lot of time, so could we get started?"

A brief shadow of hurt crossed Jim's face at Zane's words. Anna had seen the same expression last night, when Zane and his father had met outside Sarah's room.

Zane had serious issues with his father. Did he believe his father was guilty?

"I'm ready when you are," Jim said. "I missed work today to be here."

"Do you object to Ms. Wallace being in the room for the interview?"

Jim's blue eyes snapped to hers. "Not at all. Not at all. I'd be honored."

Anna smiled, but disapproval rolled off Zane in waves.

"Go on in," he told his father.

As Jim entered the small interrogation room, Zane turned to Anna.

"You are not to speak on the record. If you've got something you just can't stand to keep quiet about, raise your hand and I'll turn off the recorder. But try to just sit there and listen. If there's any problem, you're out. Understand?"

"Of course. I can sign a nondisclosure agreement if you like."

Zane's smoky gaze assessed her as his mouth turned upward just slightly. "I trust that won't be necessary?"

"I'm used to keeping secrets." She regretted the words as soon as they were out of her mouth.

Zane's gaze sharpened and he looked her up and down. "I'm sure you are."

He held the door for her to enter the interrogation room.

Jim sat stiffly. He'd placed his pearl-gray Stetson on the table in front of him and was fiddling with the rattler tail that dangled from the silver rope hatband.

Anna noticed that his hands shook. She wondered if Zane saw it.

Zane pulled out a chair and nodded at her, so she sat. He grabbed another chair. He looked cool and professional, but she could feel the tension radiating from him.

In fact, she didn't think she'd ever felt this much tension in a room. She tried to make herself invisible. She had to know what was going on between Zane and his father.

Zane turned on the tape recorder and went through the required information quickly.

"Mr. McKinney, where were you between seven o'clock and seven-thirty on the night of Sarah Wallace's murder?"

Jim fiddled with his hatband.

"Please stop that. The rattling will interfere with the tape."

"You remember when I got this big boy's rattles? You and Sloan and I went on that camping trip over to Sandy Creek?" He smiled at Anna. "He slithered into our tent."

"Just answer the question."

Jim nodded and clasped his big weathered hands on the table. "Where was I? Like I told you last night, I was having dinner at home."

Anna was sitting on the same side of the table as Zane, so she saw his left hand clench into a fist in his lap.

"Was your wife with you?"

Jim hesitated a fraction of a second. "Yes."

Anna glanced at Zane's profile. Had he picked up on Jim's hesitation?

"You and Mom—Mrs. McKinney had dinner together."

Jim looked down at his hands. "Stella had already eaten. She was in her room. I heard the television."

*Her room.* Did they not share a room? A bed? Jim was a big, vibrant, attractive man. Had Stella banned him from their marriage bed? Anna felt a growing sympathy for Jim McKinney. He was responsible for his actions, but she couldn't help thinking that his family was judging him a little harshly. And she was having a hard time picturing him as a murderer.

"So she can't verify that you were home." Zane was pushing. In a courtroom the defense would have objected, claiming *asked and answered*.

Jim looked up. "She could. I don't know if she will."

"Did you kill Sarah Wallace?"

Smoky blue eyes met slightly darker ones. Jim sat up straight. "No, I did not."

"What were you doing at the inn that night?"

"I heard she was murdered and Carley was injured, so I went over to offer my help."

"Had you had any contact with her, either that night or earlier?"

Jim frowned. "With Sarah? Didn't she go to Vegas after her mother was killed?"

"Just answer the question."

"I hadn't seen Sarah Wallace in sixteen years."

Zane unclenched his fist, although his jaw still worked. "Where were you on the night of Lou Ann Wallace's murder?"

Jim's jaw dropped. "What's that got to do with this?"

"Come on, Dad—" Zane's jaw clamped. Anna could see the muscles working. He was the Ranger, interrogating the suspect. He hadn't meant to call him Dad.

He sucked in a deep breath. "The two murders are virtually identical. It stands to reason that they're connected. I'm asking everyone to account for their whereabouts on both occasions."

"Well, you know my answer to that. I'd been drinking—a failing of mine. I don't remember where I was. Last I remember I was sitting in the living room and downing shots of Jack Daniel's."

"What time was that?"

"Around eight."

"And you don't recall staggering through the Matheson Inn just a short while before Lou Ann was found?"

Jim shook his head.

"That will be all for now." Zane turned off the tape recorder and stood. "Okay. You can go."

Jim stood. "Son?"

Anna felt Zane stiffen, saw his jaw clench again. "Yes?"

"Get by to see your mother. She's pretty upset about Sarah Wallace's death."

"I can see why she would be."

Anna stood up and held out her hand to Jim. "Mr. McKinney, thank you."

Jim bent over her hand and kissed it lightly. She thought she heard a sniff from Zane.

"Anna, words can't express how deeply sorry I am for your loss." He nodded at her, then seated his hat on his head and left the room.

As soon as Jim left, Anna turned to Zane. "Well, that was painful to watch."

He wiped a hand down his face and took a long breath. "What are you talking about?"

"You were rude and gratuitously mean to your father."

"No, I wasn't."

"Yes, you were. If you conducted all your interviews like that you'd have a personnel folder full of complaints."

"I have never had a complaint about the way I do my job."

"My point exactly."

"So you're defending the one man in Justice who is the most likely to have killed your mother and your sister."

Anna looked into Zane's eyes. Behind the stoic professional demeanor, she thought she detected a glimmer of sadness. "I guess I am."

"Why? Did he dupe you with his charm?"

"Your father didn't kill them."

Zane's gaze sharpened. "How do you know that?"

"I *don't* know it. But he was a Texas Ranger. I can't believe he's a murderer."

"Well, I can." Zane scowled at her. He didn't want to have this conversation. Anna's intrusion into his case was getting out of hand. Now that the interview with his father was over, he couldn't believe he'd actually agreed to let her sit in.

Well, not again. He'd have to find her something else to do. He thought about telling her she could go back to Dallas, but the idea of letting her out of his sight sent alarm bells ringing through his head. Two separate break-ins told him she was in danger, probably from the killer.

"I don't believe you," Anna said.

"Don't believe me? About what?"

"That you really, in your heart, believe your father committed these murders."

"My *father* is a two-bit lothario whose affairs crushed my mother and destroyed our family."

"That's a long way from murder. You really are prejudiced against him. Why not just go ahead and arrest him?"

Zane regretted his outburst. What was it about her that made him say things he'd sworn to himself never to talk about?

"Just one little reason. Evidence. Just like when your mother was killed, there's too little evidence to hang a murder charge on."

"Who saw him at the Matheson Inn that night?"

"The night of your mother's murder? Carley Matheson. She was watching TV in the lobby—"

The cowbell over the door to the station rang furiously. It was Donna Hendricks.

He winced. She was here because he'd ignored her. He hadn't sent anyone to take her statement.

Beside him, he felt Anna perk up. He almost smiled. She was obviously a reporter. She could smell a good story.

"Anna, wait for me out here. I need to talk with Donna Hendricks alone."

"I want to sit in."

He shook his head and gave her a stern look. "No. Not this time."

Her eyes widened and she swallowed. She obviously knew she wasn't going to win this battle.

"Fine," she whispered as Donna breezed by the reception desk and straight back to where they were standing.

"Hello," Donna said. "Dianne, right?"

"It's Anna, Mrs. Hendricks."

Donna waved her hand dismissively. "Of course. Zane McKinney, I've been waiting for someone to contact me about my statement."

Zane watched Anna walk through the reception area toward the coffeepot.

"Come in here," he said to Donna, opening the door to the conference room. "I'll take your statement right now."

Donna sashayed past him. Her figure in the obviously expensive silk pantsuit was trim and shapely. If it weren't for the carefully made-up bags under her eyes, the spidery veins across her nose and the deeply scored lines between her nose and the corners of her mouth, she'd have been an attractive woman. But her battle with alcohol and drugs was clearly etched into her face.

She frowned as she glanced at the chairs, then ran a finger across the wooden seat of the nearest one. After inspecting her fingertip for dust, she sat primly, her legs together and crossed at the ankles, her hands composed in her lap and an expectant look on her face.

Zane sat down across from her and turned on the tape recorder.

"Do we really need that?" Donna asked. "I hate the way my voice sounds on those things."

Zane shook his head slightly. "Sorry, Mrs. Hendricks. I have to have a record of our discussion."

"You shouldn't have dismissed me last night."

"I apologize. But I had two crime scenes and not enough people to keep them secure."

"Well, what I have to tell you will save you a lot of time."

Zane assessed her. "That would be nice."

"I thought you'd appreciate it. Leland does not have an alibi for the night of Sarah Wallace's murder."

Zane sighed inwardly. She'd said the same thing the night before. "Mrs. Hendricks, we have Mr. Hendricks's statement."

"Well, he's lying!"

"All right. How do you know this?"

"Because I saw him."

Zane rubbed his temple. She was giving him a headache. "Why don't you start at the beginning, Mrs. Hendricks. Tell me what went on that night."

"Certainly. I was working on paperwork in the office of my diner when my co-owner Rosa Ramirez came in and told me that Leland had called. He'd asked her if we had any pecan pie. We'd run out earlier in the day."

"Why would Rosa report Leland's dessert cravings to you?"

Donna lifted a manicured hand and patted her perfectly coiffed red hair.

For the first time he noticed her hand—beyond the silk nails and the rings. The long fake nails made her hands look slender, but in fact they were broad and sturdy. He had a vague memory from his childhood, watching the local rodeo. In her day, Donna Taylor had been quite an accomplished barrel racer. That took strength, more strength than one would expect, given her expensive efforts to look young and elegant. He took out his PDA and made a note.

"What are you writing?"

Zane smiled. "Just a note to myself. Try the pecan pie."

Donna beamed. "You always were a flirt, Zane McKinney. A lot like your father."

Swift anger coursed through him. *No.* He was nothing like his father. He composed his face and tamped down his feelings. "You were going to tell me why Rosa reported Leland's call to you."

"Because she has instructions to report to me about anything and everything Leland does."

Zane frowned. "Why's that? Y'all have been divorced for—what?—seventeen years. Why so much interest in your ex-husband?"

Donna's hand clenched into a fist and she brought it down on the wooden table—hard enough to bounce the tape recorder. "Because he kidnapped my baby—*his own* baby! He was broke. He'd been ruined in the oil crash. He let my little boy be murdered—" she paused and touched the corner of her eye, as if to wipe away a tear "—just to try and get his hands on the life insurance policy *he'd* taken out."

She sucked in a sharp breath. "I want to know every move he makes. I want to make his life a living hell, like he made mine. And someday I want to prove that he did it. And when I do—" She looked at her fist, and consciously relaxed it. Then she raised her gaze to Zane's. "Every day I want to kill him."

"Mrs. Hendricks, I'd like for you to write out your statement about Leland's involvement in your child's disappearance. I want you to take your time and give me every detail you can remember—"

"I remember everything."

"But do that later, when you've calmed down. Right now we need to focus on why you think Leland has no alibi."

"Chef had just taken some pecan pies out of the oven, and I was sick of all the paperwork. I decided to get out of the office for a while and deliver Leland's pie myself."

She dreamed of killing him every day, and yet she personally delivered his pie. Zane didn't think he'd ever seen a weirder relationship.

"What time was that?"

"Oh, probably about ten after seven."

"Did anyone go with you?"

"No."

"Meet anybody? Wave at anybody? Talk to Leland?"

She shook her head.

"You do realize that leaves you without an alibi, too."

She didn't even blink. "Rosa knows what time I left and what time I got back."

"Okay. I'll talk to Rosa. Now, back to Leland."

"When I got to his house, I saw him running across his backyard, toward the inn."

"Are you sure it was him?"

"Please. I was married to him for fourteen years. I am absolutely certain."

"How was he dressed?"

She hesitated. "In black. I can't tell you specifically what he was wearing. But I can tell you where he was heading. He was going to the Matheson Inn to kill Sarah Wallace."

## Chapter Five

Anna hadn't lasted ten minutes in the reception area. The coffee was old and burned, and the magazines were old and dog-eared. And of course in such a small town, the interrogation room didn't have one-way glass. She couldn't even watch Zane questioning Donna Hendricks.

She'd toyed briefly with the idea of wandering into the sheriff's office, just to see if there were any interesting files lying in plain sight, but the office door was closed and anyhow the transcriptionist was right there, speed-typing on the computer at the reception desk.

About the time Anna reached the end of her patience, the cowbell over the door rang. It was Zane's mother.

Anna smiled at her.

"I can smell that nasty coffee already,"

Stella McKinney said. "I can understand the deputies, but I don't know how Carley can stand it."

"Mrs. McKinney," Anna started.

"Call me Stella."

"Stella, Zane is interviewing Donna Hendricks."

"That's all right. I was just going to see if he wanted to come for dinner." Stella looked at Anna. "Oh, Anna, I'm so sorry. You must be devastated, and look at you. I'll bet you don't have a change of clothes. You hadn't planned on staying, had you?"

"I'm fine, really." Anna smoothed her hands down the front of her blouse. She'd given it a lick and a promise with the iron provided in her room, but it still looked like it had been worn for two days.

"Come with me. We don't have a lot here in Justice, but there is a discount clothing store. It's only a couple of blocks back to the house. We'll get the car and I'll take you shopping."

Anna didn't know whether to be grateful that Stella had offered to help her find some clothes or embarrassed that she was so obviously in need of help. She decided to take it as a sign. She wanted to know more about Zane. Plus, she needed information about the best place to make arrangements for Sarah's burial. She smiled at the smaller woman.

"Thank you, Stella. I'd really appreciate that." As she followed Stella out of the police station she took a deep breath. "You must be so proud of Zane."

Stella sighed. "Of course. I'm proud of both my boys. It's why I've stayed with my cheating bastard of a husband, for their sake."

Anna raised an eyebrow. It was hard to believe that those bitter words had come from the tiny, delicate woman's mouth.

"And it's why I haven't killed him yet."

It was after five o'clock in the afternoon when Stella dropped Anna off at the door to the inn. Anna had three new outfits, including a black dress that would be suitable for Sarah's funeral. She also had the name of the director of the Graves Funeral Home.

As she passed the front desk and nodded at Richie, it occurred to her that the he was the person most likely to know the comings and goings in the inn. She didn't know if he'd been interviewed, but even if he had, in her experience, people never told everything to the police.

She needed something to do—some way to help find the person who had killed her sister. If Zane had his way, she'd be cowering in her room, waiting for his careful, methodical approach to yield up an answer.

But she couldn't sit still and do nothing. It was why she worked in the field rather than behind a desk writing op ed pieces on issues like global warming and stock market trends.

So as soon as she deposited her shopping bags in her room, she ran back downstairs.

Richie had his elbows on the polished wood counter, playing a game on his iPod.

"Hi, Richie."

He started and looked up, then fumbled with the ear buds. To her amusement, his face turned red.

"Uh, hello, Ms. Wallace. Did you— can I—?"

Anna decided to put him out of his misery—or perhaps increase it. She leaned against the counter and gave him a conspiratorial smile. "I guess you see a lot, working here until midnight."

He shrugged. "Not so much. Justice is pretty dead most of the time. Oh, dude! I mean, ma'am, I didn't mean to say—"

"It's all right, Richie. I was wondering, though, if you could tell me a little about Sarah? Weren't you here when she checked in? Did you see her again?"

Richie nodded eagerly. "She got here about five. Went to her room. About an hour later, she called the desk and asked where she could get some food. I told her the diner was her only choice on a Sunday evening. So I ran out and got her a turkey sandwich."

"Did you tell Lieutenant McKinney or his deputies about this?"

Richie ducked his head. "I forgot, until you asked me."

So someone could have sneaked into the inn while Richie was fetching Sarah's sandwich. But what about the time difference?

"Richie, how long were you gone?"

"Not long."

"Come on, Richie. You're not going to get into trouble. You might have seen the murderer."

His self-conscious manner changed to excitement. "Seriously?"

She nodded gravely.

"Well, I did eat a couple of doughnuts and drink a big glass of iced tea while I waited for her sandwich. I got back here about six-thirty and took the sandwich to her room. She was fine then. I swear!"

"I believe you. Did you see anyone? Anyone at all?"

Richie shook his head. "You think whoever killed her was hiding in the hotel? You think they sneaked in while I was getting the sandwich? Oh, man!"

"Richie, what else?"

"By the time I gave her the sandwich, I had to pee. But that only took a couple minutes." He stopped fiddling with the ear buds. "I might have seen Rosa."

Anna's pulse sped up. "Rosa Ramirez? Did you tell anyone?"

"I just now remembered it. I came out of the john and somebody was leaving through the back door."

"How did you know it was Rosa?"

"The hair. Her hair's black and she pulls it back real tight."

"What did she have on?"

"I'm not sure. Probably something black, like usual."

"Could you tell where she'd come from?"

He shook his head. "She was in a heck of a hurry. I barely saw her."

"But you're sure it was Rosa. So who made the sandwich for you at the diner? Not Rosa."

He shook his head. "New girl. Kinda hot, if she wasn't so skinny."

"So you didn't see Rosa in the diner?"

"Nah."

"But how did she get out through that door? Isn't it locked?"

"It's like—a fire door, dude, I mean, ma'am."

Which meant that anyone could open it from the inside.

"Ms. Uh—ma'am? Do you think Rosa killed that lady?"

Anna shook her head. "No, I'm not sure the time fits. It's possible she might have seen someone."

She smiled sweetly. "Thanks. You've been a big help."

As she spoke, the lobby doors opened and Zane marched in. A pleasurable tingling at the base of her spine surprised her. It wasn't desire. It couldn't be. Zane McKinney hated her. To him, she was merely a job, and not a pleasant one, either. Anna figured he saw her mother every time he looked at her.

She brushed aside the regret that notion planted inside her and watched him walk across the lobby.

His broad straight shoulders telegraphed his confidence, his gray-blue eyes were clear and honest, and his straight mouth and strong jaw exuded determination. She'd hate to be a criminal pursued by this Texas Ranger. She wouldn't stand a chance.

Zane glanced at Richie. As soon as the kid stuffed his ear buds back into his ear and slouched against the counter, he stepped close to her and bent his head.

"I told you to wait for me. Where the hell have you been?"

"Wait until you hear what I found out from Richie."

His eyes turned stormy. "We've got to establish some ground rules here. Number one, you do as I say. And number two, you answer my questions."

Anna propped her fists on her hips. "How about number one, you explain rather than command?"

"How 'bout you tell me where you disappeared to."

"I went shopping."

"Shopping?" Zane's voice rang with exasperation. "Where? How'd you get there? I told you to wait for me. I told you I'd take you."

"Your mother drove me." She watched the wind go out of his sails.

"Mom?" Shock tinged his voice. "*My* mom? How did that happen?"

"She came to the police station to see you, and before I knew it she'd whisked me off to the clothing store."

He smiled grimly at Anna's choice of words. "That sounds like Mom. She's good at manipulating people, but—" He stopped and took a deep breath. "So you had a nice shopping trip with my mother. Can we get back to business? Because I'm ready to hear everything—and I mean everything—you know about what Sarah had for you."

Anna looked beyond him and saw Richie slip the ear buds out of his ears. A man she didn't recognize was descending the stairs. She leaned closer to Zane. "Do you really want to have this conversation here?"

He sent a quick glance around. "No, I don't. Are you hungry?"

"Am I what?" He'd surprised her. But she realized she was hungry. *Very.* She hadn't eaten anything since noon the day before. No wonder the coffee at the police station had turned her stomach.

He must have seen her answer in her eyes, because he put his hand at the curve of her back. "Come on. Let's get something to eat and you can tell me all about Richie's exciting revelation."

AFTER THEY'D BOTH cleaned up a bit, Zane drove them to Calhoun City, to a place called

Monte's. Anna recounted for him what Richie had told her.

He was beginning to get used to the way her face lit up when she was excited or interested in something. Tonight she'd worn her hair down. It fell, sleek and shiny, just to her shoulders. He still couldn't see any makeup, but her eyes sparkled like emeralds and her cheeks were pink. She practically glowed.

He'd already noticed her outfit. How could he not? She had on some kind of swirly skirt that left her legs bare. Her arms were bare, too, in a bright pink top that hinted at the delicate shadow between her breasts, and she carried a little sweater thing.

She looked flirty and elegant at the same time. He picked up his wineglass and saluted her. "So, is that one of the outfits you bought today?"

"Yes. You confiscated all the clothing I brought with me." She smiled.

He sent her a brief smile. "None of your clothes look like that. I mean—you look nice."

Her cheeks heated up and she looked down at her water glass.

Zane watched her slender finger with its unpainted nail slide around the glass's rim, and wondered why she was hesitating.

She glanced up at him through her lashes, then looked back at her finger. "It was sweet of your mom to take me shopping."

Zane didn't speak. But he did wonder how long Stella McKinney had held her own with the woman sitting across from him.

"Your mother is very bitter."

"Ya think? That's old news. Who can blame her, after what my father put her through."

"She told me about your half brother. The son your father had with another woman."

"That's old news, too," he said gruffly. "Although I'm surprised she told you. She never talks about Cole."

"Zane, your mother said she wanted to kill your dad."

A very old wound opened painfully inside him. "I know. She says things like that. Sometimes she gets overwhelmed by it all."

"I'm sorry. I just thought you ought to know." The look she gave him was filled with pity. He bristled.

"Yeah, well, now I do." He swallowed and put a lot of effort into toning down the edge in his voice.

"Listen to me, Annie, I'm glad Mom took you shopping, but you can't be running around like that. I've got to know that you're safe, every minute. You have to promise me you won't go anywhere—and I mean *any-where*—without notifying me."

Her delicate brows lifted. "Does that just apply to leaving the hotel? Or should I inform you each time I go to the bathroom?" She took a sip of wine, never taking her eyes off his face.

He was sure the greenish sparkle he saw was amusement. "This whole investigation would go a lot faster if you'd stop being so difficult."

Anna set her wineglass down. "Difficult? Okay. I'll stop being *difficult* if you'll involve me. Let me in on the investigation. I'm good at getting information from people. Look what I got from Richie that Deputy Spinoza missed."

Zane nodded reluctantly. "That was impressive. But how was he so sure it was Rosa he saw?"

"I've been asking myself that same question. He kept talking about her hair. How it was black and, as he put it, all slicked back."

"Easy to imitate. It could have been a wig, or even a black watch cap."

"We'll have to question Rosa."

*We.* Zane suppressed a grimace. No way was he letting Anna in on the investigation into her sister's murder. He couldn't afford to put her in more danger. Plus there was still that niggling certainty that she was hiding something from him. Something vital to the case. He couldn't be absolutely sure that she would tell him everything she learned. He had no doubt she would check out every tidbit herself first.

But he'd already ruffled her feathers by calling her difficult. He certainly wasn't going to mention that he considered her less than trustworthy.

Leaning back in his chair, he crumpled his linen napkin and set it beside his plate. "Deputy Spinoza took Rosa's statement today. I'll check on what she says she was doing. Are you ready to go? I've still got a bunch of paperwork to finish."

"Sure. This was a wonderful dinner. How did such a great restaurant wind up out here?"

"It's for the locals. Monte Gates grew up in Calhoun City."

"And he doesn't care that he could be making millions in Dallas?"

"Some people would rather stick close to their roots."

"At least some people have roots."

Zane heard the longing and regret in her voice. Oddly, just like when he'd questioned her last night, he felt a kinship with her. He knew how she felt, although his situation was vastly different. She'd lost her family—tragically. He had a family, he just didn't feel like a part of it.

As they walked out of the restaurant, Zane slipped his arm around her waist, sensing that she could use some comfort, denying that he might be seeking comfort for his own loneliness.

The ride back to Justice was quiet and pleasant. About halfway it started to rain, one of those slow sprinkles that could last all night.

Zane felt more relaxed than he could remember being in a long time. The constant dull ache in his temples was gone. His shoulders and back weren't so stiff. And he'd actually enjoyed his meal. When was the last time he'd actually savored good food with an attractive and interesting companion? He sent a sidelong glance toward Anna and found her watching him.

When their eyes met, she looked down at her hands, a tiny smile lighting her face. "It's raining," she said.

"Yeah. Maybe it'll cool things off." His mouth quirked as he turned his attention back to the road. He wasn't sure what either of them had to smile about, but it felt good.

At the inn, he walked her up to her room. "Here you go. I'll wait until I hear your dead bolt before I leave."

Anna unlocked the door then turned toward him. Her smile nearly took his breath away.

"Thank you, Zane. That was just what I needed. It was good to relax for a little while."

He tore his gaze from her mouth. Nodding, he gestured toward her door. "You'd better go on in. Get some sleep. Tomorrow is going to be a busy day."

"Oh, right. Who are we interviewing tomorrow?"

Zane angled his head. "*We* aren't interviewing anyone. Let me remind you, you are not involved in this investigation."

"But you let me—"

He cut her off with a gesture. Letting her sit in with his dad had been a calculated effort to throw Jim McKinney off guard. He wasn't about to include her in any other interviews. "No more, Annie. You're a witness—that's all. Besides," he hesitated for an instant, "you have arrangements to make."

Her smile faded. "For Sarah's funeral." She took a shaky breath. "Do you know when you'll be releasing her?"

"Not yet. I'm hoping it will be sometime tomorrow. Where are you planning to—"

"Bury her? Here in Justice, next to my mother." She squeezed her eyes shut for an instant. "Sad legacy, isn't it? Mother and daughter, both murder victims, buried side by side."

Zane surprised himself by touching her hair. "I'll get him, Annie. Whoever he is."

"Thank you." Her eyes glistened with unshed tears as she put her hand on his forearm and leaned in, lifting her head to press a kiss to his cheek.

His skin burned where her soft warm lips touched. He took a step backward. "Lock your door. I'll wait."

"Aren't you going to bed?"

"Like I told you, I've got paperwork to catch up on. I'm going to the police station."

She nodded and stepped into her room. "Thanks again for the evening. Good night."

Zane stood there until he heard the metallic click of the dead bolt. He glanced at the door to his room, next to hers. But as tired as he was, he'd told Anna the truth. His paperwork was piling up. He should have spent this evening going over statements and the deputies' reports from the crime scenes instead of indulging in a relaxing dinner with a beautiful companion.

He reached out and touched Anna's door, then stalked down the hall to the staircase, checking his watch. After eleven.

Was it too late to call Sloan? Before he finished the thought he'd already answered his own question.

He didn't care. He needed to find the records from Lou Ann's murder and the disappearance of Donna's child. And as Carley had said, Sloan would know where they were.

He dialed his brother's cell phone as he headed back to the sheriff's office. By the time Sloan answered, Zane was sitting in Carley's desk chair and staring out the rain-streaked window at the dark parking lot behind the inn.

"McKinney," his brother growled.

"Don't tell me you're asleep."

"Damn close. What the hell do you want?"

Zane grinned. Sloan had never liked to be woken up. It had been one of the delights of Zane's life to pounce on his younger brother's bed first thing in the morning, just to hear him squeal. "Well, it seems to me that if you've got time to go to bed early, you should have time to get over here and help me with this case."

"Not for a few more days," Sloan said on a

yawn. Zane heard fabric rustle as Sloan sat up. "You caught me asleep because this is the first chance I've had in two days."

"My heart bleeds."

Sloan huffed. "Did you call for some particular reason or just to harass me?"

"Where are the case files relating to Lou Ann Wallace's murder and Justin Hendricks's disappearance?"

"Have you got something?" Sloan's voice turned razor-sharp.

"Not yet, but the deeper I get into this, the more ob-vious it is that Sarah Wallace's murder is connected with her mother's murder sixteen years ago."

"All those records were gathering dust, and mice were beginning to nest in some of the boxes, so I pulled them and sent them to Dallas, to the Archives."

"Great. I'll request them. Listen, Squirt, get your butt over here as soon as you can. I can't relate to these people the way you can."

"Maybe if you'd shed that poker you've got stuck up your—"

"Nice talking to you, too. I'll call you later."

Zane disconnected and leaned back in the desk chair. He'd cut Sloan off, but he'd gotten the gist of his comment. He cursed quietly.

He would never be an easygoing, hand-shaking hometown boy. He was too stiff, too by-the-book for such a small town. Sloan, on the other hand, had the people of Justice wrapped around his finger.

Zane just hoped his brother could make the townsfolk open up, because he sure couldn't.

ANNA TOSSED HER PURSE and the little beaded sweater onto the bed and kicked off the low-heeled sandals Mrs. McKinney had helped her pick out.

She flopped onto the bed without turning on the lights and scrunched a pillow up under her head. She couldn't believe she'd kissed him. She grabbed another pillow and covered her face. If he hadn't already been convinced that she was a younger, flakier version of her sister, he surely was now.

"Why did I do that?" Her question echoed in the room. She had no idea, except that the thought of burying her sister—the last of her family—had blanketed her with a profound sadness. And Zane had been so kind, so sweet, comforting her.

That was it. She'd just responded spontaneously to an act of kindness. It didn't mean anything.

Then why was his scent lingering in her nostrils, reminding her of how close he'd stood to her nearly naked body last night? Why was the newly shaved smoothness of his cheek still tingling on her lips?

"Argh!" She tossed the pillow aside and got up. She didn't even like Zane McKinney, and he certainly didn't like her. In fact, given the way he felt about her mother, it must have been hard as hell for him to be nice to her for a whole evening.

Although he had seemed a lot more laid-back than she'd seen him so far. From the first time he'd spoken to her in Sarah's room, she'd gotten one overarching impression of him. From his focused, methodical questions, to his demeanor, to the way he carried himself, he exuded control. Until tonight. Tonight he'd seemed at ease. In different circumstances, they might have been on a date.

Only the circumstances weren't different, and he'd probably rather shoot himself than go out with her. She pressed her palms against her temples to stop the argument that rattled in her head.

The clock on the bedside table read eleven-thirty. She was exhausted, but she knew she wasn't going to get any sleep tonight. She got up to change into the camisole pj's she'd bought this afternoon.

Instead, she found herself reaching for a pair of jeans. She wasn't really going to leave the hotel. All she was going to do was see if the diner was still open. It was nearly midnight, so it was doubtful. Still, she'd like to have a cup of hot chocolate. And if she was lucky, she might run into Rosa Ramirez.

She grabbed her purse and slipped downstairs. A young woman she didn't know was working the registration desk. Richie must be off tonight. The girl was slouched on the stool, eyes glued to a small TV on a shelf behind the desk.

Anna crept across the lobby, her running shoes making no sound. About three steps west of the lobby doors was the retro glass-and-chrome entrance to Donna's diner, so close Anna hardly even felt the rain. The lights were off in the front of the café, and the sign on the door had been flipped to Closed.

It was hard to picture the society-conscious Donna as the owner of a two-bit diner in a small Texas town. It would be interesting to know why she'd bought it—certainly not money. Donna's father had left her plenty.

Anna caught a movement at the back of the café, behind the counter, where the lights over the griddle and the fryer baskets served as night safety lights. She squinted. It was Rosa and Donna. Rosa had her hands propped on her hips and Donna's arms were crossed. It looked like they were having an argument.

Donna flung her hands out in an "I give up" gesture and turned her back on Rosa, reaching for her designer purse and shaking her head.

Rosa grabbed her arm and got in her face.

Anna could vaguely hear their voices, but not what they were saying. Rosa's voice was shrill, Donna's more controlled.

Finally, Donna tossed her head and marched toward the door, her head down as she dug in her purse for her keys.

Anna backpedaled, her pulse hammering, then turned and ran back toward the lobby entrance. She stood in the corner of the west door. If Donna were headed for the hotel, Anna would be caught. She racked her brain for a harmless reason she'd be sneaking around the lobby at midnight.

To her relief, Donna stalked straight out to her car, her purse held over her coiffed head. After she'd pulled away, Anna crept back over to the diner door. Rosa was wiping down the counter and muttering to herself.

Anna pushed on the door. To her surprise, it opened.

Rosa started and her head jerked up.

"Hi, Rosa." Anna winced at her timid voice. She cleared her throat. "Rosa. I'm Anna Wallace."

Rosa clutched the damp cloth to her breast. "I know who you are. You are sister to Sarah Wallace."

Anna put on her concerned journalist face and smiled reassuringly. "That's right."

"And daughter to Lou Ann Wallace." Rosa spat her mother's name. "It is past time to close. There is nothing hot. I can give you a donut or a piece of pie to take back to your room."

"I'm not here for food, Rosa. I need to ask you some questions."

Rosa's black eyes held undisguised suspicion as she frowned at Anna. "It is late. I must get home."

"This will only take a minute."

"I have given a statement to Luis. I have nothing more to say."

Anna sat down at the counter and picked up a couple of books of matches out of a bowl. "You didn't mention to Luis that you were in the hotel last night, around the time my sister was murdered."

Rosa folded the dish towel she held in half, then half again, then smoothed the edges with her fingers. "I was not."

"Richie, the desk clerk, saw you."

"That is impossible. I was here. What does that one claim he saw?"

"He says he saw you going out the back door sometime after seven o'clock."

"He lies."

"He also says he didn't see you here in the diner when he picked up a sandwich a few minutes earlier."

"I was dealing with paperwork in the office."

Anna twirled one of the matchbooks in her fingers as she looked at the wooden door behind Rosa. "May I see the office?"

"No! Miss Donna doesn't allow anyone in there." Rosa folded her arms and glared at her. "You leave now. I am locking up. I work early tomorrow."

"When my mother was murdered, your fingerprints were found in her room, weren't they?"

Rosa's black eyes snapped. "I worked as maid in the inn. My fingerprints were in every room. I know nothing of Lou Ann Wallace, except—"

Anna leaned forward. "Except what?"

Rosa continued to fold and unfold the towel she held. "She was your mother, so I don't like to—"

"I know what my mother was like. Please tell me what you know."

"I know nothing. Just that your mama, she break Miss Donna's heart, two times over. Two times!" Rosa gestured.

"She married Leland. That must have hurt Donna."

"*Sí*, but not so much as losing her baby."

"Her baby?" Anna's breath caught in excitement. Had Lou Ann been involved in the disappearance of little Justin Hendricks? Because if so, that would go a long way toward explaining why she'd been killed.

Rosa sighed and draped the dish towel over the edge of the counter.

"Rosa, tell me about the baby."

But Rosa had said all she was going to say. She shook her head. "Miss Donna is not so strong as everyone thinks. She is still sad from losing her child." She reached around her and untied her apron. "Now I am going home and you must leave."

Anna stood and hiked up the purse strap that had slipped down her shoulder. She stuffed the books of matches into her jeans' pocket as Rosa came around the counter to herd her toward the door.

Anna paused in the doorway. "Rosa, if you know anything about my sister's murder or my mother's, you need to tell us. If you weren't involved, nothing will happen to you."

Rosa put a hand on Anna's back and pushed her through the door and locked it.

FINDING HERSELF looking down the narrow alley between the inn and the diner, Anna thought about the placement of Donna's office and Richie's mention of the fire door. Didn't all places of business require fire doors—those heavy metal doors that could be locked from the outside, but that had a panic bar on the inside to escape in case of fire or other danger?

If she could just get a look at how close Donna's office was to the back door of the lobby, she'd know whether Rosa had had time to get over to the inn, kill Sarah and slip back without anyone knowing she'd been gone.

Of course she'd have to have a way to get in through the locked door. Anna took a couple of steps into the alley.

Something rustled beside her. She jumped sideways, her pulse thrumming in her temples. Standing perfectly still, she listened as whatever it was squirmed noisily. Then a dirty orange head popped up from a trash can.

*A cat!* It scrambled out, nearly knocking over the metal can, and shot down the alley, splashing through a few puddles that the rain had made.

Anna took a long, relieved breath. "Come on, Wallace," she whispered. "You're an investigative journalist. Investigate!" She stuck her hand in her pocket and encountered the books of matches. She didn't even remember pocketing them.

Digging one out, she flipped up the cardboard cover as a plan began to form in her brain. She could use the matchbook cover to keep the fire door from locking.

She turned and headed into the lobby. The girl at the desk was still absorbed in a late-night talk show and painting her fingernails. She didn't look up.

Anna walked right past her, but instead of turning toward the stairs, she kept on going, toward the back door. Looking back over her shoulder, she realized that the fire door couldn't be seen from behind the registration desk. It was only visible from the middle of the hall.

Quietly, she pressed the metal bar and

pushed the door open. Slipping through, she slid the matchbook cover into place between the door latch and the striker plate, and carefully closed the door.

Then she looked around the deserted back of the building. Two sconces on either side of the fire door provided just enough light to create long eerie shadows and wet, shiny reflections on the asphalt.

Several yards west was the side wall of the diner. Anna glanced around her. Everything was quiet now that the rain had stopped, nothing but crickets and the occasional hoot of an owl.

She slipped across the short expanse of parking lot to the back of the diner. Sure enough, there was a door, right where she'd expected it to be.

It would have been a snap to block the door locks, then, when the time was right, sneak out of the office and run across to the inn.

Rosa could have killed Sarah. As Anna retraced her steps to the inn's back door, another thought occurred to her. Her discovery implicated Donna, too.

She reached for the doorknob with one hand and caught the corner of the matchbook with the other. Her purse strap slipped off her shoulder.

She heard a rustling behind her. The cat again? She hunched her shoulders and quickly turned the knob.

Somebody yanked her purse away, bending her wrist painfully, then a knee in her back shoved her against the door and gloved hands wrapped something around her neck and jerked it tight.

Anna tried to scream, but she could barely breathe. Tried to fight, but her struggles just pulled the strap tighter.

"What did Sarah tell you?" The harsh whisper rasped in her ear.

"I—can't—breathe—" Anna's voice was a nearly soundless croak.

The choking hold loosened slightly. "Tell me."

"N-nothing," she gasped.

The strap tightened again, cutting off the last of her breath.

"You're lying."

Anna tried to twist around, but she couldn't. She tried to dig her fingers in between the garrote and her neck, but the killer's hold was too tight.

"Can't—breathe—" She croaked as her lungs spasmed and a million stars swam before her eyes.

"Tell me what she told you or you'll die."

## Chapter Six

Zane grabbed his Colt .45 automatic from the hook by the back door as he rushed outside, heading toward the scuffle he'd spotted through the window of the sheriff's office.

The attacker cut and ran toward the woods.

"Halt!" Zane shouted, sparing a glance at the small unmoving form that had crumpled to the ground where the attacker had shoved it. He tasted the sharp tang of fear. Had the killer claimed another victim?

"Texas Ranger," he shouted. "Halt or I'll shoot!"

The dark-cloaked figure didn't stop. He crashed through the underbrush and into the tangled, overgrown woods without even slowing down. Zane took off after him, pushing through the underbrush.

Finally, Zane stopped to listen, trying to get a bead on which way the fugitive had gone, but the crunching of foliage and snapping of twigs faded almost immediately. Whoever it was had an intimate knowledge of the wooded area. Zane didn't.

*Damn it.* He'd lost him. He should have taken the shot before the guy reached the woods, but he never fired his weapon indiscriminately. Too late now. Knowing he'd just be wasting time trying to follow the culprit into the thick underbrush, he turned and sprinted back to where the victim lay sprawled on the ground. Her hair and clothes were lit by the inn's rear door lights.

*Annie!* His heart slammed painfully against his chest wall. He knew that soft dark hair, those slender arms. "Oh, God, don't let her be hurt."

He knelt down and touched the delicate skin of her throat, searching for a pulse. It beat light and fast under his fingertips. His hand trembled with relief.

"Annie!" As he brushed her hair away from her face, he saw for the first time that her purse strap was wrapped around her neck, just like Sarah's had been. His heart thudded with apprehension.

The thing he'd feared since he'd first seen

her had come to pass. Sarah's murderer had targeted her.

"Annie, can you hear me? Come on, wake up." He caressed her head and swept her hair away from her face with one hand while he pulled out his cell phone with the other. He speed-dialed Jon Evans.

The doctor's voice was rough with sleep.

"Jon. Anna's been attacked. We're at the back door of the inn."

"I'll be right there."

Just as he pocketed his phone, Anna stirred and groaned.

"Hey, Annie."

For a split second she froze, then she flailed her arms, trying to push him away. "No! No!"

"Annie! Annie, it's me. Zane."

"Zane!" She sat up and flung herself into his arms. He wrapped his arms around her and pulled her close.

Thank God she was okay! As fear for her safety began to fade, he became hyperaware of her soft breasts pressed against his chest, her sweet-smelling hair tickling his nose, her shallow, frightened breaths warming his neck.

His brain sent alarm bells ringing all the way through him. What was he doing? He'd never been much for touching and hugging.

In fact, as a law-enforcement officer, he shouldn't be touching her at all. He should be assessing her for injuries and trace evidence.

But he didn't want to let her go. He had to stop this before he quit thinking like a Ranger.

He wrapped his fingers around her upper arms and set her away from him. "Careful, Annie. Stay still. Dr. Evans is on his way. We need to be sure you're not injured."

Her hand went to her throat. "I'm not—"

"Shh. Don't talk, and try not to move. I want Jon to check you out thoroughly."

"It was the killer," she whispered. "He asked me what Sarah told me."

"You heard his voice? Was it a man?"

She shook her head. "I don't know. Whoever it was came up behind me and grabbed my purse and—" She shuddered.

"Okay. Shh. We'll wait for Jon so you only have to tell it once. How do you feel? Are you hurting anywhere?"

"Just my throat. Did you see him?"

Anger pulsed through him. "For a few seconds. He seemed to have on some kind of cloak or long coat. And a hood or floppy hat. Whoever it is knows what they're doing. I couldn't tell if it was a man or a woman."

"You didn't catch him?" Her voice was raspy and tight with fear.

Zane cursed. "No. He's got a huge advantage over me. He—or she—knows those woods like the back of their hand. He may even have a bunker set up back in there somewhere."

Anna turned her head and looked at the woods. Her shudder rippled through him.

"Do we have to stay out here?" she said in a small raspy voice.

"Just until Jon gets here."

She nodded and wrapped her arms around herself. Zane's heart melted at her brave vulnerability. He ought to be asking her what she was doing out here alone. Later he'd be furious at her for putting herself in danger. But right now all he could think about was how close she'd come to being killed, and how much that scared him.

ANNA SAT ON THE OLD lumpy couch in the break room of the police station as Dr. Evans examined her neck. "I don't think your larynx is bruised." He placed his fingers over her throat. "Swallow for me. Does that hurt?"

"Not much. How long do you think it's going to take Zane?" she asked.

Dr. Evans smiled at her. "He doesn't want to lose any possible evidence, so he's walking the area searching for anything that might lead to the attacker. He'll be back in a few minutes. Now hold this ice pack on your neck."

Anna took the ice pack just as Zane came in. "Did you find anything?"

"Nothing but the clasp to your handbag." He held up a small plastic bag containing a gold-colored button. "I guess I'll run it for prints, but I doubt we'll find anything. Whoever attacked you didn't leave any evidence." He looked at her neck, frowning. "Was he wearing gloves?"

Anna thought about the shocking instant when she was pushed against the door and her purse strap was wrapped around her neck. "I think so, but it all happened so fast..."

She moved to place the ice pack against her neck.

"Hold it. I want to test for fingerprints first. It's a long shot, but I can't ignore anything that might give us a clue."

Zane retrieved a couple of sheets of fingerprint paper from one of the crime scene kits and pressed the sticky film against each side of her neck. He talked as he worked. "I saw a couple of places where dust and gravel were disturbed as he ran off toward the woods, but that parking lot is cracked and uneven, and it's too dry to get a shoe print."

"Those woods have been a menace for years," Evans said. "Not only do we get rats and snakes and roaches because they're so close, but kids think the underbrush and the grapevines are perfect for playing Tarzan. We had a little boy get lost back in there a few years ago. He apparently fell into some kind of underground cave."

"Cave? Here in east Texas?" Zane sounded surprised. "I played in those woods when I was a kid, but I never saw a cave."

Evans shrugged. "Well, you know—it was probably more like a limestone outcropping or a bluff that a kid might call a cave. He finally heard the searchers calling him and followed their voices. Everyone was so relieved that he was alive that nobody went back to search for the cave."

Zane tipped his chair back, balancing on the two back legs. "A cave in the woods. I'm thinking the underbrush and bugs and darkness would eliminate most women from the suspect list."

"Not really," Anna said. "I loved exploring when I was a kid. Of course we lived in Vegas, so my 'jungle' consisted of alleys and garbage bins and vacant buildings, but the premise is the same."

Anna pressed the ice pack to her neck,

shivering at the cold. "Dr. Evans, who in Justice would have the most knowledge of those woods?"

"I guess that would be the people who've been here the longest—who grew up here."

Zane's chair legs hit the floor. The look he shot her warmed her chilled skin. It was filled with admiration and approval. "Annie's onto something, Jon. Help me figure this out." He stood and walked over to a chalkboard mounted on the wall. He picked up a piece of chalk and wrote *Suspects* on one side and *History in Justice* on the other.

"Okay, who's been here longest?"

"Donna Hendricks grew up here," Jon said. "She and her family lived in the Matheson Inn."

Zane wrote her name and next to it, wrote *all her life*. "Somebody mentioned that Leland worked at the inn when he was a teenager. Do you know when he moved here?"

Jon shook his head, so Zane wrote *Leland Hendricks* and beside his name wrote *teenager* followed by a question mark.

"What about Rosa?" he asked.

Anna hardly remembered Rosa. She shook her head.

"Seems like she's always been here. She

was Donna's housekeeper for years before they opened the diner together," Jon commented.

Zane wrote Rosa's name and beside it printed *since Donna's marriage to Leland*. "Okay, who else?"

Anna met his gaze, hating what she was about to do. "Your parents?"

A shadow passed over his face. Her heart squeezed. She didn't want to think that Zane's father might have attacked her, but she knew he belonged on the list. And she knew Zane knew that, too.

He turned his back on her and wrote *Jim McKinney*. Beside his father's name he wrote *all his life*.

"You were born here?" she asked.

He nodded without turning around. "He and my mother met while he was with the highway patrol. She grew up around San Antonio." Below Jim's name he wrote Stella's and *since marriage to Jim*. Then he set the chalk down and dusted his hands together. "I guess that's the short list. Is there anyone we've missed?"

"Most people in Justice grew up here. It's that kind of town. Both Matheson and his wife, the Enises…" Jon ticked off the names on his fingers.

"But nobody else that we know of who was closely associated with Lou Ann."

The doctor stood. "Well, I've got to get home. I'll have my report for you tomorrow." He turned to Anna. "Are you sure you don't want something for pain or to help you sleep?"

She shook her head. "Can I take this ice pack off my neck now? I'm freezing."

"Sure. You're going to have some bruising, but a scarf or a turtleneck should cover it."

"Good idea, Jon. I don't want anyone to know you were attacked, Annie, not even the deputies. It might come in handy to see how fast that news travels."

Zane stepped close and examined her neck. "Jon, given the imprint of the purse strap, what can you tell me about her attacker?"

"Stand up." The doctor held out his hand. Anna took it and stood. He turned her around so her back was to him.

"She was at the door so she had to be standing on the concrete stoop. For the attacker to get a good grip, he would have been right behind her."

"He put his knee into my back," Anna reminded them.

"Then he grabbed her purse strap between

his hands, giving him two strips of leather to use to strangle her, like this."

Jon slipped an imaginary purse strap around her neck, fisted his hands and demonstrated pulling. "I'm about the same height as Anna, so the bruise I'd leave would angle downward."

"The same for anyone who was her height or smaller," Zane said. "So, are we eliminating anyone who is taller than her?"

"Not necessarily. Someone very strong and trained in such tactics could actually pull downward to mislead."

"Right." Zane gently pushed her hair out of the way and studied her neck intently. Anna felt his warm breath on her nape. "What about Lou Ann and Sarah?"

"Sarah was prone, so all the killer had to do was roll her onto her stomach and stand over her or straddle her. You won't get any indication of height from Sarah's bruises." Jon glanced apologetically at Anna.

She shook her head. "It's all right."

"I assume Lou Ann was also on the floor when she was strangled."

Zane let go of her hair. "Thanks, Jon. Don't mention any of this, okay?"

"No problem. Good night, Anna." Evans left.

Anna swallowed. It hurt. She coughed quietly and reached for her purse.

"What are you doing? That's evidence." Zane scowled at her as he stopped her hand.

Anna gave him an innocent look. All she wanted to do was to get inside her room so she could shiver and shake and break down without anyone knowing. "Going back to my room. I'm really tired."

"Are you sure you feel all right?" His expression didn't change but his voice sounded worried.

She sent him a shaky smile. "I'm okay. I want to thank you—"

He planted himself directly in her path. "I'm glad you're okay, because I want to know what the *hell* you were doing out there."

So much for a clean getaway. She sighed. "I wanted some hot chocolate, so I went down to the diner. It was closed, but I saw Rosa and Donna having an argument."

"You wanted hot chocolate? I waited outside your door until I heard you lock it. Why do you think I did that?"

Anna swallowed and bit her lower lip.

"Because I didn't want to leave until I knew you were safe in your room."

"I talked to Rosa."

Zane threw his hands out in a gesture of helplessness. "You let yourself be trapped in an unfamiliar place with a murder suspect?"

"Listen to what I found out. She lied about being in the lobby Sunday night."

"You expected her to own up to it?"

"The fact that she lied implicates her in Sarah's murder."

"Everybody lies, Annie."

The lift of his brow told her he included her.

"So you went to the diner. How did you end up being attacked behind the inn?"

She clutched his forearm. "That's what I'm trying to tell you. Rosa said she was working in the office in the back, behind the counter. It occurred to me that there was probably a fire door in the back of the diner, like the one at the back door of the inn. It would be easy as pie for someone to sneak out of the diner, into the inn and back out."

The lines between Zane's brows smoothed out. His expression turned thoughtful. "The fire door locks from the outside."

Anna grinned at him, even though it hurt her neck. "That's right. But if you're clever—" She dug in her jeans' pocket. Hadn't she picked up more than one matchbook? Her fingers finally closed around it. She held it up triumphantly.

"I went through the lobby of the inn and out through the fire door. Then I slipped this between the latch and the striker plate and voilà, I had free access to the inn from outside."

Zane folded his arms and stared down at her.

She cleared her throat. "Then I walked across to the back of the diner. Sure enough, there was a door."

"So you strolled around in the dark in the middle of the night with a murderer on the loose. And before you could get back inside to safety, you were attacked."

"Something like that," she muttered.

Zane's breath whooshed out in an exasperated sigh. He thrust his fingers through his hair and paced back and forth for a few seconds before stopping directly in front of her.

"Do you understand that you nearly died out there?"

"But, Zane—"

He grabbed her upper arms. "No! Don't say another word. How am I supposed to conduct my investigation when I have to spend all my time worrying about you?"

His face was mere inches from hers, his blue eyes smoky and intense. His hold on her arms loosened and his thumbs skimmed her sensitized skin as his gaze slid down her jawline to her neck.

"You don't—" She started, but her voice was swallowed up by the pounding of her heart. "You don't have to worry about me."

He touched her neck with a surprisingly gentle fingertip. "Look at this. Of course I have to worry. If something happened to you I'd—"

Anna raised her head, meeting his gaze. His eyes lingered on her lips as his fingers slid around the back of her neck.

She melted inside, overwhelmed by his gentle touch, his quiet, caring words, the naked yearning in his eyes.

Reality tried to break the spell his tenderness had cast. *Not him,* her brain scolded. Not Zane McKinney.

His father had killed her mother. She had every reason to hate him and no reason at all to trust him. She pulled away from his hypnotic touch.

"I'd better get back to my room," she said hoarsely.

"No."

The spell was definitely broken. Zane straightened and stepped backward. "You're not going anywhere. I obviously can't trust you out of my sight, so you're sleeping here."

"Here? How does that help anything? My room is not fifty paces from here, and it has a bed and a bath. Plus your room is right next door."

"Forget that. I want you where I can see you."

"No. That's out of the question. Look at me. I'm covered with dust. My clothes are ruined. I need a shower."

"You can clean up in the bathroom here."

"And where am I going to sleep, in the jail?"

Zane's mouth twitched. "The thought crossed my mind, but you'd probably be more comfortable on the couch in the break room." He shrugged. "Besides, unlike the inn, the front and back doors of the police station have double dead bolts. The only way anyone can get in or out is with a key."

"This is outrageous. Who can I complain to about your harassment of me?"

"That would be me. I'm in charge of this investigation, which means I'm in charge of everything."

Anna considered her options. She could make a break for it, but undoubtedly Zane would overpower her. She could call somebody and complain, but Zane was right about that, too. Who other than him was there to call? Besides, she was still terrified by her attack. She wasn't sure she could stay alone tonight.

And the idea of Zane watching over her while she slept was irresistible.

## Chapter Seven

Zane got Anna settled in on the couch. There were a couple of blankets in the supply closet and a pillow that had definitely seen better days.

"Are we going to do this every night?" she asked, her voice soft and husky with sleep.

He smiled. "If we have to."

"I can't stop thinking about what Dr. Evans said about the rats and snakes and roaches." She shivered.

"They're better than the human vermin who're after you."

"Where are you going to sleep?"

"I'll stretch out on the cot in the holding cell. If you need anything, call."

Anna pulled the blankets up to her chin. Her eyelids were drooping with exhaustion. "Thank you, Zane."

"No problem."

He turned out the light, leaving only the red and blue lights from the soft drink machine. They cast an ethereal glow on Anna's dark hair and outlined her delicate features in rainbow hues. She glimmered like an angel.

Zane shook his head at his fanciful thoughts. "The lights going to bother you?"

She shook her head. "I like them. They remind me of my room in Las Vegas. The casino lights shone in our window all night long...." Her voice trailed off.

Zane stood there for a few minutes watching her. She fell asleep immediately, her breathing soft and even in the silence. In the dim light with the blankets covering her, he couldn't see the marks on her neck. But he knew they were there, and knowing that brought him as close to losing control as he'd ever been.

He wanted to go out and drag in every single person who might have hurt her and beat the truth out of them. Immediately, he suppressed his irrational thoughts.

Thinking like that wasn't going to help him catch the killer. Neither was becoming emotionally attached to Anna. Hell, her mother destroyed his family.

*She's nothing like her mother.* The thought whispered through his brain, mocking his self-described professional detachment.

Resisting the impulse to smooth a wayward strand of hair out of her face, he turned on his heel and stalked down the hall to the holding cell and lay down on the lumpy cot. He bunched up the worn-out pillow and stuck it under his head.

The fact that he hadn't been able to catch Anna's attacker galled him. Could he have caught him if he'd chased him into the woods? If he hadn't turned back to check on Anna?

He thought about the tangle of brush, vines and trees, thinking about what Jon had said about the bluffs and outcroppings back there.

If the attacker had a hiding place in that wild overgrown area, it was going to be hard as hell to find him.

There was only one thing he could do. Zane cursed under his breath. He had no choice. He needed the best tracker in Texas, and that was Sergeant Cole McKinney of the Texas Rangers. The bastard son of his father, Jim McKinney. Zane punched the pillow again and turned on his side, but his mind still raced. Acutely conscious of Annie asleep just a few feet down the hall, he resolutely closed his eyes. Finally, he drifted off to sleep.

ZANE WOKE UP to a loud banging on the front door.

*Annie!* He vaulted off the cot and rushed up the hall to the break room.

Anna was just stirring. She pushed her tangled hair out of her face. She looked at him, her green eyes soft and heavy-lidded with sleep. "What is it?"

"Someone's at the door."

She jumped up. "I'll get the blankets folded."

Zane nodded and headed toward the front door, bemused by his instinctive reaction, and by hers. Why were they both intent on hiding the fact that they'd slept together in the police station?

*Because this is a small town,* he answered himself. It didn't matter if he'd locked himself in the jail cell and she'd locked herself in the bathroom, people would still talk.

He opened the door. It was Jon.

"Morning, Zane."

Zane squinted at the doctor in the early morning sunlight. "Morning," he said gruffly.

Jon laughed. "I guess I woke you up.

I brought you something." He handed Zane a paper bag. "Celia sent Anna a couple of scarves."

Zane took the bag. "Thanks, Jon. You're a good friend. Tell your wife how much I appreciate this."

"All part of the job. Well, I've got early clinic hours today. I'd better get going."

"Jon—"

"I know. Nothing about the attack. I'll keep my eyes and ears open. Maybe if we're lucky, the killer will come in to be treated for scratches and poison ivy."

Zane laughed. "That would help. Thanks again, Jon."

He closed the door and went back to the break room. Anna wasn't there, but he heard water running in the bathroom. He set the sack down on the break table and stepped across the hall to Carley's office, checking his watch. It was early, but state offices opened early.

He flipped through Carley's Rolodex until he came to the number for the State Department of Archives and History. After quickly keying the number into his cell phone, he pressed CALL.

Within a few minutes, and helped by a judicious mention of his position and his captain's name, he'd arranged to have the case files for Lou Ann Wallace Hendricks and Justin Hendricks pulled.

"We can overnight them to you," the receptionist said.

"That's not fast enough. I'll send a deputy to pick them up this morning."

Back in the break room, he found Anna finger-combing her hair and yawning.

"How's your neck this morning?"

She lifted her chin. "It looks awful. I didn't realize it was so bruised."

Neither had Zane. The sight of the blue and purple double stripes across her delicate skin sent fury burning through him.

He picked up the sack. "That was Jon at the door. His wife sent you this."

Anna took it and looked inside. "Scarves." She smiled up at him. "Dr. Evans is a good man."

"Yes, he is."

She pulled out a pastel square with shades of blue and green and lavender and a red oblong scarf. Then she looked down at her pink T-shirt. "Well, the blue and lavender one matches my bruises."

She folded the pastel scarf and knotted it around her neck. "Is everything covered?"

Zane stepped up close to her and touched

the scarf, spreading the edges to conceal the array of blue and purple marks on her neck. Her scent affected him like pheromones. Just being close to her, just taking in her essence, turned him on with an intensity that he'd never felt with any of the women he'd dated.

He stopped fiddling with her scarf and slid his fingers up along her jaw. She turned her head toward him, her lips moist, her breathing shallow.

Zane skimmed his mouth across hers, as softly as a butterfly's wings, and a tiny gasp escaped her lips. She looked up at him, then her gaze drifted downward, to his mouth.

He responded, his need immediate and fully rigid. How long had it been since a woman's warm breath and the lightest touch of her lips had caused him to burn and harden like a randy teenager?

With no thought other than the exquisite anticipation of tasting her, he covered her mouth with his and cradled her head in both hands. She responded, fisting her hand in his T-shirt and reaching up to kiss him back.

He probed with his tongue, urging her to take him in. She accepted his deeper kiss and their tongues met.

Zane felt as if fireworks were exploding inside him. His entire body was aflame with desire, and if he could judge by the supple melting of her body against his, she felt the same way.

When both of them were breathless and he was aching with unslaked need, he pulled back slightly and rested his forehead against hers.

"Annie," he whispered.

She closed her eyes and lifted her head until her nose rubbed against his. "Zane, I—"

"Well, well! Lookee what I found."

Zane jerked and stepped backward, dismay flooding through him.

*Damn it.* It was Burns. As much as Burns resented him, he could just imagine what the deputy would do with this little discovery.

Anna smiled, although her cheeks were bright pink. "Good morning, Deputy. Lieutenant McKinney was just showing me how my sister was strangled."

Burns's eyes glittered as he took in Anna's tangled hair and wrinkled jeans. Zane wanted to wipe the leering grin off his face.

"Is that so? As I recall," Burns drawled, "the evidence placed the attacker *behind* the victim."

To her credit Anna didn't lose her cool. She took a step backward. "He was pointing out the difference in height of Sarah and the person who attacked her."

"Deputy, what's on your agenda this morning?" Zane interrupted before Burns could come back with a crude remark.

"I reckon I'll check with the lab on those prints we lifted, and finish processing the stiff's—beg your pardon, ma'am—the victim's belongings." Burns paused, looking at Anna and Zane. He frowned. "Why? What's going on?"

Zane wasn't about to tell Burns about Anna's attack. He didn't want anyone to know about that. It could be a useful piece of information to hold back, to see if anyone in town mentioned it on their own.

"I need you to drive into Dallas this morning, to the Department of Archives and History, and pick up the case files on Lou Ann Wallace Hendricks and Justin Hendricks."

"Justin Hendricks?" Burns looked bewildered for a few seconds, before recognition dawned. "I remember now. Donna's kid. The little boy who went missing back then."

"Right. Now get going. I need those files this morning."

Deputy Burns gave Anna one more leering look, then touched the brim of his hat. "Yes, sir, boss. I'm on my way."

Burns left with a clanging of the cowbell over the door.

Zane met Anna's gaze. "The deputies have keys. I apologize. That won't happen again."

Anna's legs weren't doing their job. They were trembling, just like the rest of her. She sank down onto the couch. Zane's kiss had rocked her world. She'd had boyfriends, even a couple of semi-long-term relationships, but she'd never been kissed like that.

"Are you all right?" Zane asked, looking at her quizzically.

She nodded and swallowed. "Fine. I'm fine. I guess I was more affected by the attack than I realized." What else could she say? She couldn't tell him that his kiss had left her a dozen times more shaken than last night's attack.

And what did that reaction say about her? Deadly attacker. Deadly kiss. Boy, were her priorities mixed up.

Zane's brows lowered and his stormy-blue eyes assessed her. She could read his mind. He filed away her odd reaction and got back to business.

"I'm going to question Leland and Rosa this morning, and go over the case files from Lou Ann's murder and Justin Hendricks's disappearance. What are you going to do?"

A wave of grief washed over her. She had obligations she had to take care of. "I've got to make arrangements for Sarah. Do you know when—"

"I'll call Jon. The autopsy should be done by now. I'll have him call you with the information."

She stood. "Then I guess I'll go back to my room and clean up."

He nodded, stepping back, out of her way. "Deputy Spinoza installed swing-bar latches on the inside doors of all the rooms yesterday. Lock the door and throw the latch when you're in the room. And don't open it—don't even peek out with the latch on unless you know exactly who's there." He took another step backward. "In fact—don't open the door to anyone except me."

His concern warmed her. He seemed worried about her safety—seemed determined to personally ensure that she remain unharmed. She wasn't used to anyone taking care of her. It felt good. She felt secure, knowing Zane was watching out for her.

She smiled. "I won't." Looking up into his eyes, she caught a glimpse of blue fire. It was nearly hidden, but it was there.

She longed to stand on tiptoes and steal another taste of his mouth, but his body language told her whatever had passed between them during that kiss was filed away in an appropriate place in his brain.

Anna knew with a calm certainty that Zane McKinney never mixed business with pleasure. He'd meant what he'd said. It wouldn't happen again, and that left her with a deep, unfulfilled longing.

ZANE DROVE OUT to Leland's estate and caught him having breakfast under a canopy beside his pool. He was dressed in gold silk pajamas and a Chinese print robe. He offered to order breakfast for Zane but Zane declined. He did accept a cup of coffee, though.

"Jamaican Blue Mountain," Leland said. "I have it flown in weekly. Thirty dollars a pound."

Zane nodded. "It's good." Good, but not worth thirty bucks. It looked like Hendricks was living high off Lou Ann and Justin's insurance money. Zane wondered how long it had taken for the insurance companies to pay off. Obviously, they eventually had.

"I assume you're not here just to sample my coffee." Leland grinned, his teeth white against his bronzed skin. Then just as quickly, he grew sober. "How is my stepdaughter?"

Zane's irritation level flew sky-high. He'd never liked Leland. The man was too slick, too arrogant. And the idea that he would claim Anna as his stepdaughter just so he could appear magnanimous by offering her his help really galled Zane.

"You mean, Annie?" he countered. "She's fine. Just fine."

"I do wish she'd accepted my invitation to stay out here with me. I don't get to see her enough."

"I suppose you don't. Not since she moved away sixteen years ago."

Leland frowned. "I went through a very bad time. If Anna felt neglected, it wasn't because I didn't care for her."

Zane was already tired of listening to Hendricks and his platitudes. "Leland, I need to ask you about your movements Sunday night, the night of the murder."

"Deputy Spinoza already questioned me."

Zane ignored him. "For instance, you said you were home alone that evening."

"That's right. The staff were off duty, so I made myself a sandwich and watched a movie."

"But that wasn't all you did, was it?"

Leland's eyes narrowed. "What do you mean?"

Zane set his coffee mug on the table and propped his elbows on his knees. "You called Donna's diner."

Zane felt the older man close down. His eyes turned cold, his face hardened.

"Well? Didn't you?"

"I ordered a piece of pie. Donna's mother's pecan pie recipe is sinful, but I didn't know it was a crime."

"Who'd you talk to?"

"Give me a break, McKinney. If you know about the pie, you know I talked to Rosa, and you know Donna delivered it to me."

Zane raised his brows. "I do know that. But you're leaving out an important detail."

Leland looked puzzled. "Am I? What detail?"

"The fact that you weren't at home when Donna got here with the pie."

"That she-devil is lying. Of course I was home. She drove up, brought the pie to the door and drove off."

"Can you prove that?"

"Yes. My surveillance system records everything."

*Surveillance system.* "Does Donna know about the surveillance system?"

"She's the one who wanted all those protective measures in the first place."

"So you have recorded proof that she drove up, gave you the pie and drove away. And that's all?"

"That's all." Leland looked closely at Zane. "Why?" he demanded. "What did Donna say? What did she tell you?"

Zane considered Leland. He seemed genuinely indignant that Zane would question his movements. But Donna had sounded sincere, too. Apparently the two of them were practiced liars, and they'd had years to hone their skills against each other. Their animosity was clouding Zane's case, and he was sick of both of them.

"Donna said you weren't home when she delivered the pie. She said she saw you sneaking across your backyard in the direction of the Matheson Inn."

Leland almost choked on his coffee. He set down his mug and coughed. "You have got to be kidding me. She said *that*? She's crazier than I thought she was."

"Are you telling me it wasn't you she saw?"

Leland leaned forward. "I'm telling you she didn't see anybody. The woman's a nut. And she's trying to implicate me in Sarah's murder. Hell, she probably killed her herself."

Zane sighed, frustrated. "Okay. What time did she deliver your pie?"

"About seven o'clock. I didn't look at the clock, but the surveillance disk'll have that information."

"Then get me the disk."

"No problem, Lieutenant." Leland reached for his cell phone and pressed a button. "Harry, get me the surveillance disk from Sunday night, specifically around seven o'clock. I'm out by the pool." He disconnected. "Harry will bring the disk right out."

Zane stood. He was ready to get back to the relative sanity of the police station. He'd had enough of Donna and Leland's hurtful version of *he said, she said*. At least now he had concrete evidence. With Leland's surveillance disk, he'd be able to prove or refute Donna's claim that Leland wasn't at home. Although it was odd that Donna would lie if she knew the surveillance disk was recording her every move.

Leland's employee came toward them, holding a CD case. "Here you go, boss," he said.

Leland gestured toward Zane, so Harry turned and held out the case to Zane.

"Thanks. Leland, I'll be talking with you again."

"No doubt," Leland said, pouring himself another cup of coffee. "Harry will see you out."

Zane drove back to the police station and sat at Carley's desk. He inserted the disk into the DVD player on Carley's desktop computer.

It looked like the camera was mounted on the security gate into Leland's estate, and pointed directly at the front door and the circular drive in front of it.

Zane fast-forwarded, watching the time stamp. He stopped it at seven o'clock and let it play in real time, fast-forwarding sporadically, making sure he didn't miss anything. At just about 7:02 p.m., he saw the front fender of a dark sedan pull into the drive and into the camera's frame.

Then there was a sharp crack and the screen went black.

"What the—?" Zane pressed reverse and ran that section of the disk again.

*Sharp crack. Black screen.*

*Sharp crack. Black screen.*

Had Donna shot out the camera? He couldn't tell if the noise was a handgun. For that he needed an expert's opinion. Ejecting the DVD, he put it back in the case. He'd send it to the crime lab in Garland. The graphics expert there was one of the best. If anyone could decipher exactly what had happened, Rick could.

The cowbell over the door rang and Burns walked in, carrying two file boxes.

"Here you go, Lieutenant. The case files you wanted." He piled them on the desk. "The lab had your trace done, too. I brought it all back. Here's the crime scene's lab report."

"Good. Thanks. I'm glad you're back, because I've got another assignment for you."

To his credit, Burns didn't object.

"I need you to run this surveillance disk back to the crime lab."

Burns scowled as he took the DVD case. "Right now?"

"Right now. It's from Hendricks's place. Something knocked out the camera. I want to know what it was."

"You think Hendricks is the doer?"

Zane shook his head. "I don't know. But it's a lead. And I've had few enough of those so far."

## Chapter Eight

The funeral director stood and held out his hand. "I think you've made a good choice," he said solemnly.

Anna took his hand and endured his sober smile. "Thank you, Mr. Graves. Tomorrow at ten o'clock, then."

"And you're sure you don't want visitation?"

She extracted her hand from his clammy palm and resisted the impulse to wipe it on her pants. "No. As I told you, I think that under the circumstances—"

"Quite, quite." Graves nodded.

As soon as she could, Anna escaped his dour presence. A small, sad smile tugged at her lips. Graves Funeral Home. How eerily appropriate.

She walked down the street toward the inn, feeling the eyes of the townspeople on her.

Wincing internally, she thought about Sarah's funeral. It was a given that the entire town would be there. She'd have preferred to have the service today—as soon as possible, without telling anyone about it. But Graves had tactfully pointed out that Sarah and the town deserved more. As did Anna. They all needed closure.

Anna's eyes stung. She'd cried more these past two days than she'd ever remembered crying before, even when her mother was killed. Back then she'd been too shocked, too frightened to cry.

Now she was crying for both of them, and for herself. The undertaker was right. Sarah's funeral would bring closure, not only for Sarah and the town, but for Lou Ann, too.

As she started up the steps to the inn, she saw Zane come out of the police station carrying a paper bag. The clothes he wore—jeans, white shirt, tie and cowboy boots—epitomized the man. He was professional, yet at ease with himself. Confident, yet slightly aloof.

She paused and watched him walk toward her. His long legs allowed him to cover the ground quickly without looking rushed. His broad shoulders appeared capable of carrying the whole world.

She shivered at the memory of him holding her in the darkness, pulling her into his warm, safe embrace. She'd been so helpless as the attacker tightened the strap around her throat. So weak as the garrote cut off her breath and the killer's voice whispered that she would die. Then Zane had appeared out of nowhere and she was safe.

Zane's boots echoed on the wooden steps. "Morning, Annie. Are you all right this morning?" His smoky-blue eyes studied her face and neck. She felt their heated caress like a laser, burning her skin.

For an instant she sensed that he wanted to touch her neck where the red scarf hid the ugly purple bruises, but he restrained himself.

Belatedly, she nodded. "I'm okay. I just came from the funeral home."

"Good." He climbed the last step, pushed open the door to the lobby and held it for her. "I need to talk to you."

Anna's heart leaped. "Have you found out who attacked me?" she whispered.

He shook his head and nodded toward the stairs.

Taking his hint, she didn't say anything else until they got to her room. Zane closed the door, locked it and threw the swing bar.

Anna looked at him expectantly. "Well?"

"No, I didn't find your attacker. But the crime lab in Spinoza finished processing your clothes." He held up the paper sack. "You can have them back," he said, setting it down on the bed.

"Thank you." Anna looked at the sack and thought about all the people who must have touched her blouse, her pants, her underwear. She would never be able to wash them enough to erase that memory. She'd throw them all away, except maybe the high-heeled pumps.

"When is the service scheduled?"

Anna blinked, then looked up at him. "Tomorrow at ten. I want to go ahead and get it over with as soon as possible."

"That's probably the best thing." He paused. "Listen—"

He sounded serious and hesitant. She lifted her chin. Was he about to apologize for kissing her this morning? She wasn't sure if she could bear it if he did. That brief, exquisite moment had sustained her through the embarrassing encounter with the deputy this morning, and through the painful and sad duty of arranging her sister's burial. She needed that kiss to stay in her memory as a tender gift, not a mistake.

He took a deep breath and she clenched her

fists at her sides, her shoulders tightening as if in expectation of an ambush.

"I'm not going to be able to sit with you in the family area at the funeral. I need to be out front where I can see everyone."

She hadn't realized she'd been holding her breath until it whooshed out in relief. "That's...that's okay."

He gave her a quizzical look as he continued. "It's a cinch that if Sarah's killer is someone in Justice, he will be at the funeral. Everyone in town will be there, so his absence would look suspicious."

"I'll be fine alone." She realized how pathetic that sounded when Zane's gaze softened.

He stepped closer and touched the scarf. "Are you going to be able to make a scarf work with whatever you wear to the funeral?" He gave her a small smile.

"I'll manage. When your mother took me shopping I bought a black dress. Black goes with anything."

His smile faded at the mention of his mother. "Don't take what Mom says too seriously. She's pretty fragile with all the scandal surrounding my father."

"She's been hurt. I understand that. But she's very proud of you and your brother."

To her surprise, Zane's cheeks turned pink. "Yeah, Sloan. You'll probably get to meet him soon. He's coming to give me a hand with the investigation."

He was still fiddling with her scarf. At that moment, he realized it and jerked his hand away. He rubbed the back of his neck.

"I guess I'd better get going. I've still got to interview Rosa."

Anna picked up the paper sack that contained her clothes.

*Clothes.* She had to find something for Sarah to wear. Her heart sped up as she thought about Sarah's suitcase. If Anna's things had come back from the crime lab, maybe Sarah's had, too.

Sending up a silent apology to her sister for using her to play the sympathy card, she angled her head and smiled sadly at Zane. "I've got to bring a dress for Sarah to the funeral home. Is there any chance I can have her things now?"

He didn't answer right away, but the soft light in his eyes turned hard. He might feel responsible for her, might even be attracted to her, but he didn't trust her. And why should he?

He'd had her pegged from the beginning. He'd known she wasn't telling him everything.

If he found out about the suitcase, he'd be furious at her for withholding evidence. Furious? He'd despise her.

She couldn't trust him, either. The thought made her sad, because she wanted to. Wanted it desperately. But his father could have killed her mother. And if he had, then it was highly likely that he'd killed her sister, too.

As much as she wanted to believe in Zane McKinney's integrity, he was still his father's son, his family. And family was everything.

Zane eyed Anna, wondering why she was pushing so hard to get Sarah's things. This was the third time she'd asked for them. It was possible her interest in her sister's belongings was innocent. His gut told him differently however. He was pretty sure her interest had to do with whatever she wasn't telling him. For that reason if no other, he wasn't about to let her get her hands on them, not before he'd had a chance to study them himself.

He'd glanced at the crime scene report this morning. The suitcase had yielded nothing significant. Sarah's purse, as expected, had Sarah's DNA and fingerprints on it, but no others.

"You can come to the police station," he said evenly. "I'll let you get a dress, but that's all."

"Why can't I have the suitcase—and her purse and whatever else she brought with her? She's...she was my sister." Tears welled in her eyes.

Zane told himself he wasn't moved by her distress. Then he called himself a liar.

"They've obviously been released by the crime lab. Please."

"They haven't been released by me."

Irritation replaced sadness in her olive-green eyes. She took a long breath and straightened to her full height. "Then I'll take *one dress*, Lieutenant."

ANNA SAT in the tiny viewing room next to the casket. She'd agreed to have a short viewing before the funeral. It gave her a chance to observe the townspeople as they came in to pay their respects. She wondered if Sarah would think she was perverse. She doubted it. Sarah would probably encourage her to thumb her nose at the curiosity-seekers and gossips.

Organ music droned from discreet speakers as a low chatter filled the room. Anna smiled stiffly as Donna Hendricks reached for her hand.

"Please accept my deepest condolences," Donna said as Leland approached.

"Anna, dear," he said, reaching for her other hand.

Donna shot him a look filled with daggers and let go of Anna's hand. "Excuse me, dear," she said, never taking her eyes off Leland. "It just got stuffy in here."

"Anna, you shouldn't be staying in that rat-trap excuse for a hotel. Why don't you come stay at the estate with me?"

Anna gaped at him. He'd been completely uninterested in her all these years, and now he wanted to act like the concerned stepdad? "Thank you, Leland, but I don't think so. I'm fine at the inn."

Zane stepped into the room. He had on a charcoal gray pinstriped suit with an impossibly white shirt and a gray and deep red tie. His brand-new dress shoes were polished to a mirror finish. He looked like a successful young businessman. Like a million dollars.

His gaze met hers and he sent her a sympathetic smile that lit his face and promised her that everything would be fine now that he was here.

But his gaze didn't linger. He swept the room, studying each person. Zane wasn't here to pay his respects. He was here to sniff out a killer.

Jim McKinney and his wife appeared at the

door. Jim held his Stetson in his hand. He was wearing a tan suit that looked a little too big for him, and those beautiful tooled-leather boots. Stella had on an expensively tailored dress in a deep teal blue. Her hair and makeup were perfect.

Anna glanced at Zane, who was frowning at his parents. Did he know how much he looked like his father? Both men were ruggedly handsome, with the kind of face that only gets more interesting with time. By looking at Jim, she knew exactly what Zane would look like in twenty-five years.

She was positive Zane had no idea how blatantly his love for his dad was etched on his face, not to mention his anger at him.

As Jim and Stella approached Anna, she tore her gaze away from Zane and concentrated on the two of them.

"Anna, I'm so deeply sorry about your sister," Jim said, bowing over her hand and kissing it.

A choked sound came from Stella. Her expression reflected stiff disapproval.

When Anna looked at her, she pasted a sad smile on her face.

"Hello, dear. That dress looks nice, and the scarf is an interesting choice. I'm sorry we didn't have time to go into Dallas to shop."

"Thank you again, Mrs. McKinney. It was so nice of you to help me find some clothes."

Behind Jim and Stella were several people Anna didn't know. She shook their hands and accepted their condolences graciously. Out of the corner of her eye she saw Rosa Ramirez come in.

Rosa's presence pretty much completed the circle. It was highly likely that one of the people in this room right now had murdered her sister, and probably her mother, too.

Suddenly the room was too warm, too close. She felt penned in. Her mouth went dry and her hands started trembling.

Zane saw Anna's increasing agitation from across the room. Had she seen something that distressed her? Or had the small room and the crowd gotten to her? All the color had drained from her face and her eyes darted toward the arched doorway like a horse ready to bolt.

He pushed through the crowd and reached her side just as the funeral director appeared and began to herd the guests to the chapel for the service.

"How're you doing?" Zane whispered.

He saw her throat move as she swallowed. "I'm okay, I guess. I just realized that this little room was full of suspects. That one of these people probably killed Sarah. It just spooked me."

A little color returned to her face as the room slowly emptied.

"Come on, I'll walk you around to the family room. This will all be over soon."

He put his hand at the small of her back and she leaned close as he guided her through the crowd and out of the room.

Her evocative scent—a faint aroma of strawberries—filled his head and her innocent trust filled his heart. It was getting harder and harder for him to remember that she was the daughter of the woman who'd destroyed his father's career and ripped his family apart.

After he made sure she was settled behind the lattice privacy screen, he headed back to the chapel and stood near the rear doors. He'd observed each person as they entered the viewing room. Now he wanted to study them as they filed out after the service.

It was a long shot to think that the killer would give himself away by his expression, but Zane never took chances, and he never missed an opportunity to study his suspects.

The funeral director slipped in beside him as the organ music faded and Reverend Ainsworth began to speak. His generic message centered around the value of human life, the sorrow surrounding the death of so young a woman and her unborn child and the solace found in faith.

Mr. Graves stepped closer to Zane. "Lieutenant McKinney, is the killer here?" he asked in a hushed, excited whisper.

Zane spared him a censorious glance. "Probably," he muttered. "I need you to bring Anna to me as soon as the service is over. Don't let anyone stop her to talk."

Graves's eyes glittered with excitement. "Of course. Are you going to arrest someone?"

"No," Zane said evenly, meeting his gaze. His *don't-mess-with-me* glare must have worked, because Graves turned white as a ghost and his Adam's apple bobbed as he swallowed.

"Right. Certainly. I'll just—"

Zane's gaze didn't falter.

Graves backed out through the doors and scurried down the hall, his soft-soled shoes squeaking on the hardwood floor. Zane reached out and closed one of the double doors. He wanted every single person to have to walk past him to get out of the room.

Reverend Ainsworth didn't waste any time. Within a couple of minutes he wound up the service and nodded at the organist. Funereal music swelled as he raised his arms, indicating that the people should rise and file out.

Zane straightened. His eyes studied each and every guest as they walked past him. Most of them eyed him with curiosity. The rest—Leland, Donna, Rosa, his mother and dad, the mayor—either sent him a questioning look or didn't meet his gaze at all. Richie the desk clerk hadn't attended.

About the time the last person exited, Graves appeared with Anna. Zane assessed her quickly and thoroughly. She was pale but composed.

"Thank you, Mr. Graves. I can't tell you how much I appreciate your help," she said. Her voice started out small but gained strength quickly.

Zane nodded at him and slipped his arm around Anna's waist. "I'll drive you to the graveside."

She nodded. He guided her out the back door to the covered drive. He shook his head at the hearse driver and led her to his car.

As he started his car and maneuvered it directly behind the hearse, he glanced at her. "Are you doing all right?"

She played with the clasp on her purse. "I'm fine," she said. "I'm sad—" Her voice threatened to break. She swallowed, then continued. "I'm sad, but at least she's at rest, and she will be beside our mother."

Zane clamped his jaw against the surge of compassion that rose in his chest. Her words were trite—something any experienced funeral attendee might murmur to the bereaved—but he knew by her tight, small voice that she was sincere. In fact, he was dismayed to discover how well he knew her in such a short time.

He didn't want to know her. Didn't want to feel her grief and pain the way he was right now. Didn't want to care what happened to her. He just wanted to catch the person responsible for her sister's death, wind up this case and get back to his life.

*His life.* He'd always thought he had it made. An ideal job as a lieutenant in the Texas Rangers, a nice apartment, friends and an unending supply of gorgeous Texas beauties who were more than willing to go out with him on his terms—casual fun and no strings. So why did he suddenly feel empty? Unfulfilled? Even lonely?

As he followed the hearse into the cemetery, he kept one eye on Anna. Her gaze never left the hearse as it drove around to the freshly dug plot.

Her eyes sparkled with unshed tears and those luscious lips that had quivered under his were compressed with barely controlled grief. How had he ever thought she was mousy?

Zane felt something in the center of his chest—something a lot like pain. He longed to hold her, to protect her and make sure that nothing ever hurt her again.

*What the hell was wrong with him?*

Scowling at his ridiculous thoughts, he parked behind the hearse and walked around to open Anna's door. He held out a hand to help her from the car. She took it and stood right in front of him.

"Zane, thank you—for everything," she said softly.

He dipped his head slightly, until his breath lifted a strand of her hair. "Just doing my job," he muttered as he led her to the row of chairs placed beside the grave.

"I'm going to stand back and watch everyone."

Anna met his gaze briefly, a flicker of panic crossing her face like the shadow of a butterfly. Her lips parted as if she were about to say something, then she pressed them together and nodded.

He positioned himself just on the other

side of Lou Ann's grave—the perfect position to watch the guests. Glancing down at her headstone, he saw a bouquet of dead roses. It had a card attached to it.

The card and the roses were dry, unlike the dirt and grass around the headstone. The flowers had been placed there since midnight. His pulse hammered as he debated the advisability of disturbing possible evidence or calling attention to himself.

It only took him a second to decide that he needed to get that note before someone else noticed it.

Casually but quickly, he bent down and plucked it from the withered bouquet. He wanted to pick up the flowers, too, but he didn't want to draw that much attention to either himself or to Anna's mother's grave.

Without looking at the note, he stuck it in his pocket. Then he dug out his cell phone and called Deputy Spinoza, who was on duty at the police station.

"Spinoza, is there a florist in town? Check with them. Get the names of everyone who has bought red roses in the past six months. Ask them how long it takes long-stemmed roses to die, because they look like they've been dead a long time. After you talk to the florist, get out here to Lou Ann Hendricks's grave and collect these flowers as evidence. And don't mention this to anyone."

He pocketed his cell phone and turned his attention to the arriving guests. The graveside service drew fewer attendees than the indoor service had. The skies were overcast and there was a hint of rain in the air. He hoped Spinoza could get the flowers before it rained.

As the cars pulled up and people got out, Zane stepped about twenty paces away from Lou Ann's grave. He wanted to see people's reactions as they approached the most notorious gravesite in the cemetery and saw the dead bouquets that hadn't been there the day before, and hadn't been alive for a long time. He didn't want them distracted by his presence.

Leland Hendricks got out of his Lexus, smoothed his coat and tie and stepped carefully over to the row of chairs. As he approached, his gaze slid to Lou Ann's grave, and his brows knit together in a frown. His eyes flickered toward Zane as he sat down next to Anna.

Jim and Stella arrived in the same car, and both spotted Zane immediately. He nodded slightly at them. Jim's gaze swept past Lou Ann's grave and paused briefly on the dead roses. It made sense to Zane that his dad wouldn't miss so obvious a clue. He ignored the irritating voice that whispered in his head—*guilty, guilty.*

Stella's face was a mask of long-suffering disapproval as she took in Lou Ann's grave, flowers and all. But her attention quickly turned to Jim, and she tugged on his arm and whispered something to him. They sat in the second row.

Donna and Rosa arrived together. Rosa's black eyes darted toward Lou Ann's grave and her expression indicated that she was faintly surprised. She quickly and surreptitiously crossed herself, then slid into the second row.

Donna looked at Zane first, then at the grave. Her expression didn't change, until she turned toward the chairs. She glared at the back of Leland's head as she sat next to Rosa in the second row of chairs.

About a dozen more folks showed up, but Zane didn't know most of them. Both Deputy Enis and Deputy Burns were there. They sat in the last row, with their hands on their guns.

Reverend Ainsworth kept the graveside service short. He soon wound up his last prayer, and everyone stood and began to disperse.

Zane headed for Anna's side as well-wishers lined up to speak to her. As soon as Zane got close enough, Anna tucked her hand inside his elbow.

Leland stood and waved his arms. "Everyone! Everyone!" he shouted. "I'm having a light lunch—just finger food—at the estate. Please come by."

His gaze lit on Anna. "Anna, dear. Please come by," he said. "Everyone will want to pay their respects. I don't know why you didn't have visitation last night, but that's okay. We can make up for it at lunch."

Anna didn't speak. Her fingers dug into Zane's arm with surprising strength.

"Sorry, Leland. There are some things I need to go over with her that can't wait."

Leland's face turned dark red. "Anna—?" It was less a question than an implicit command.

She leaned closer to Zane. "I'm sorry, Leland. But as Sarah's *stepfather,* I'm sure you can handle the guests. I have to concentrate my time and energy on finding her killer."

"But...but—" he sputtered. His glare demanded Zane's cooperation, but Zane wasn't about to subject Anna to something she so obviously didn't want to do.

He shook his head at Leland, then led Anna through the crowd, holding on to her as she endured the endless saccharine condolences and hugs.

Finally they reached his car. He helped her into the passenger seat and climbed in the driver's side and started the engine.

"Thank you."

"Just doing my job," he tossed out.

*Like hell,* he countered to himself. He'd have liked to hear what everyone said to her, but the note in his pocket was already scorching the wool gabardine, and he knew its contents were more important than anything anyone would say to Anna in his presence.

Still, that wasn't the real reason he'd rescued her from a long drawn-out afternoon of feigned sympathy and curious looks.

It was obvious that she was only seconds away from her breaking point. Her sad eyes and straight, vulnerable shoulders ripped at his heart.

"I know," she said, her voice quavering, "but I don't think I could have stood it much longer."

"I got that impression." He stopped in front of the double doors to the Matheson Inn. "Here we are. I'll walk you to your room."

*Her room.* She cringed at the idea of being

in there alone with her thoughts, her regrets, her guilt. But it was obvious Zane was itching to get away from her. So she nodded.

As she dug in her purse for the key to her room, Zane's warm hand left her back and he fished his cell phone from his pocket. It vibrated in his hand.

She unlocked her door and stepped into her room, feeling a twinge of relief that it looked just like it had when she'd left this morning.

"McKinney." Zane spoke into his phone.

She set her purse and keys down on the bedside table. The spring-loaded tension of the morning dissolved into tremors. She sunk to the bed, exerting superhuman strength to keep from totally collapsing, her limbs were shaking so.

"Hey, Jon. What's up?" He paused, listening. "You did? Just now?"

He met her gaze, and the smoky-blue of his eyes turned to storm clouds. His jaw clenched. "Yeah, right here."

A shard of fear lodged in her chest. Whatever Dr. Evans was telling him, it wasn't good. "Sarah's autopsy?" she choked out.

Zane didn't answer, but he stepped closer to her, his expression grim. "Are you sure? Sorry. Of course you are."

He took a sharp breath. "Right. Don't give that information to anyone. Not even the deputies." He paused. "I'm sure. I will, if she needs it. Thanks, Jon."

He disconnected and pocketed his phone, his gaze directed somewhere toward his shoes.

"It is Sarah, isn't it?" She moved to stand, but her legs wouldn't hold her up.

Zane put a hand on her shoulder. Its warmth seeped through to her bones. "You need to relax. You're exhausted. I want you to promise me you'll rest."

"What did Dr. Evans find?" She pushed his hand away and stood unsteadily. "What?" she demanded.

He grabbed her by her upper arms. "Annie, come on. Take a deep breath. Calm down."

Panic tried to steal the last of her breath, but Zane's soothing voice pulled her away from the edge. She nodded shakily. "What's happened? It's bad, isn't it?"

"Jon got the results of Sarah's autopsy. Annie—she was pregnant. Only a few weeks."

## Chapter Nine

*She was pregnant.* Zane's voice echoed in her ears—over and over. *Pregnant.* Pregnant.

"Sarah—?" That shard in her breast cut so deeply it nearly doubled her over. "Sarah was going to have a baby? Oh—"

The pain was too much. Too sharp. Too dreadful. She felt herself falling. Her vision went black. Her ears rang.

Then strong arms caught her and she was hauled up against a hard-planed chest and held gently as a low, sweet voice rumbled through her.

*Zane.* It was Zane. Somehow he'd rescued her from the abyss. She let herself be held, protected, as her brain slowly processed the awful truth.

Her sister had wanted to start over—start fresh. She'd said so in her note. And now

Anna understood. She'd done it for her baby. And for Anna, just like she'd said on the phone. *I've missed you, Anna-banana. I want to be a family again.*

"Oh, Sarah," she whispered. "I should have known."

"Hey, Annie." Zane's low voice hummed in her head again. "How're you doing?" He leaned back a little to look down at her. "You going to faint on me again?"

She shook her head. Tears welled in her eyes. "Did he say—about the baby. Could they tell—?"

"Jon said he was a little boy."

Anguish clogged her throat. The empty place inside her grew. "If I'd been nicer to her on the phone, she'd have told me. We could have…we could have buried him, too."

"You did," he whispered. "He's there with his mother. Annie, you did everything you could."

She shook her head, dislodging tears that made dark circles on Zane's coat lapel. She touched one with her finger. "I'm ruining your coat—" Her breath caught in a sob.

Tenderly and quickly, Zane lay her down on the bed and took her shoes off.

Anna rolled onto her side and curled up into a fetal position. Tears trickled across the bridge of her nose and onto the pillow.

Zane cleared his throat. "Annie, I need to get back to the police station. I'm expecting a call any minute."

She nodded without opening her eyes. "Go ahead," she whispered. "I'm fine."

She was so far from fine. Zane could see that in the tight curve of her body in on itself and the way she'd clung to him. His arms felt empty, useless, now that she was no longer in them.

Her arms were scrunched against her chest, her fists clenched. She'd been through so much in her life. Losing both her mother and sister to a murderer. And now, finding out she'd lost a nephew who'd only existed for a few brief weeks. The child had been murdered, too. Now she truly was alone.

"Zane?"

He barely heard her. Her voice was slurred with drowsiness and muffled by the pillow.

"Can I go with you? I just don't want to be alone now."

He slid a finger under a strand of hair that had fallen across her cheek. *Like silk.* He smoothed it back, away from her face.

Her heavy-lidded gaze pleaded with him.

"Tell you what, Annie. I'll stay here until you fall asleep."

"Don't want to sleep. I want to be with you."

A surge of unexpected desire surprised him. Her quivering lips, the vulnerable curve of her back and shoulders, the slight shadow that was barely visible between her breasts— all called to his most primal instincts. To protect her. To shield her. To claim her as his in the most intimate way he knew how.

What a heel he was thinking about sex. Especially right now. Her fragility, her vulnerability, radiated from her in waves as hot as a midsummer highway. They called to him.

*Protect.* That was his job. To protect her. And he knew he couldn't leave her alone.

He crossed to the other side of the bed and slipped off his shoes and jacket. Then carefully and silently, he lowered himself onto the bed. Scooting over, he lay behind her, spoon-fashion, close enough to drape his arm across hers and rest his chin on top of her head. Not close enough that she'd know how aroused he was.

They lay like that for a long time. Zane couldn't believe how relaxed he felt, lying with her. He'd be mortified if she discovered how his body was betraying him. Worse, she'd hate him for lusting after her while she grieved.

He dozed off a couple of times. His arousal still throbbed, but it was a sleepy, manageable desire. At least, although he still ached with want, he wasn't experiencing the painful burning lust that had engulfed him earlier.

Then she moved. He came fully awake as he realized she was turning to face him.

He pulled away and composed his face.

She tucked her hair behind her ear. Her eyes were puffy from crying. Her scarf was askew, revealing the dark bruises on her delicate neck.

"Thank you for holding me," she said as her lashes swept down then back up. Her voice was husky, raw with the emotion she was trying so hard to hide. "I apologize for being such a wimp." A wry smile curved her lips as dampness glittered in her eyes again.

He brushed his knuckles along her petal-soft cheek. "Don't. You've been through a lot. Everybody has a breaking point. You reached yours, and nobody can blame you for grieving over your sister and her baby."

"Do you?" she whispered, trailing her fingers lightly over the inside of his wrist.

His pulse quickened. "Blame you? No, of course not."

She shook her head. "Have a breaking point."

*Yeah.* And he was about there. His erection pressed painfully against the inseam of his slacks. He needed to get up, get away from her. Go find the professional detachment that he lost when he was around her.

He shrugged one shoulder. "Everybody does," he said tightly. Her fingers were driving him nuts. She'd abandoned his wrist and was caressing his thumb and the sensitive skin of his palm. He pulled his hand away from her cheek.

"So you have? When?" She slid her hand up his forearm, past his elbow and on to trace his bicep.

"Annie—" His erection throbbed. His pulse hammered in his ears. *Her mother destroyed his family. His dad might have murdered hers.* Not even those awful truths could distract him.

She moved closer. Her hand left his bicep and traced the line of his shoulder and neck. Then slowly, tentatively, she lifted her head and reached for his mouth.

Cursing himself for being an idiot, he met her halfway. Her lips were soft under his.

And parted. He kissed her with a gentleness he had to dredge up from the core of determination deep inside his breast. Restraint did nothing to calm his racing pulse or to temper his raging desire.

Annie's fingers tightened in his hair as she raised up. He let her take the lead. As she moved above him, he lay back and allowed her to lower her mouth onto his, abandoning his effort at gentleness.

Her leg moved between his thighs and his last chance of stopping this really bad idea skittered away as she rubbed her thigh along his tight, hot arousal.

She gasped and whispered something against his lips. He took her breath and her words, and gave her his in return.

Wrapping his fingers around her waist, he lifted her atop him. At the same time he kissed her more deeply, opening up to her, reveling in her need, acknowledging his own.

Running his palms down her sides past her hips, he found the hem of her dress and slid it up, past her bottom, her waist, her little bra. She raised her arms as he pulled it over her head and off.

She shook her hair back and fumbled with the scarf's knot until she got it loose. A surge of anger tempered his desire for an instant as he gingerly traced her discolored skin.

Then he met her gaze as he slid his fingers down over the swell of her breasts and slipped them under the edge of her bra and around, searching for the clasp. He quickly undid it.

She tossed the scarf and the bra to the floor. Her cheeks turned pink as she met his eyes. He lifted her and shifted until she straddled him.

His mouth watered as he looked at her lovely body. Her breasts were small yet full and beautifully formed, their dark pink nipples distended with arousal. Her waist was slender above the lush swell of her hips. His gaze slid down to the apex of her thighs, where a minuscule scrap of lace did nothing to hide the golden-brown patch of hair.

His arousal jerked, becoming harder and throbbing with exquisite pain. Anna's eyes widened as he tightened his buttocks and strained upward, brushing against her, torturing himself.

She reached for his shirt buttons and quickly, jerkily, undid them. He let her concentrate on undressing him. He had other things to do. He slid his hands down to the tops of her thighs and farther, until his thumbs met at the tiny vee of lace. It was already damp. His breath hitched. He pushed the scrap of material aside.

Releasing his breath sharply, he slid his thumbs along her soft, slick flesh that was no longer covered by anything.

Anna moaned and shuddered, his shirt buttons forgotten.

He smiled in triumph as he watched her lips part and her eyes glisten with arousal. There was nothing in the world more beautiful than a woman aroused. Nothing more satisfying than giving her pleasure.

His thumbs never stopped their exploration—first one, then the other. He was relentless, his touch tender yet probing.

Anna's thighs tightened around his hips. "Zane—" she gasped. "Please. Don't—"

"Too late," he muttered as he found her rhythm and brought her to explosive climax.

Her body spasmed, arched, again and again. A guttural moan escaped her throat.

Clenching his teeth, he undulated against her bottom as she came. He held himself in check by sheer force of will as she crumpled, boneless, onto his chest. Then he wrapped his arms around her and turned them both, until he loomed above her. He searched her face.

She slipped her hands under his shirt, pushing it off his shoulders. Then she reached for the waistband of his pants, brushing against his arousal.

Sitting up, he undid his pants and pushed them down, along with his boxers. His arousal sprang to rigid, pulsing hardness.

She drew in a long breath as she tentatively touched him.

"Careful," he whispered. "I'm right on the edge."

She opened herself to him. He knew she was slick and ready. Carefully, so carefully, he pushed into her. Her gasp and her exquisite tightness told him she wasn't used to this. For her, it was special.

If he could have spoken, he'd have told her how special it was for him. But all his energy was concentrating on taking it slow.

Her hands grasped his buttocks and she arched, taking him deeper, breathing in short, shallow bursts.

"Are you okay?" he breathed, relieved when she nodded.

"Please," she mouthed. "Kiss me."

And he did.

Wrapped in her, seared by her smooth firm flesh, heat began to build inside him. Her lips moved as she murmured something against his mouth. Her hands still clutched his buttocks, her fingernails dug into his flesh.

He was past the point of no return. His entire being was consumed by her. He kissed her mouth and throat, and whispered her name as he thrust again and again.

Then he felt it, the arching of her body toward him, the straining, the small, sharp breaths. As he exploded into climax, his last rational thought was that she was coming, too.

Anna lay surrounded by Zane, her insides still thrumming with tiny aftershocks as her breathing began to return to normal.

He was still inside her, his waning pulses echoing her own. She trailed her fingertips along his back and spine, silently thanking him for distracting her from death and loss.

Was that what he'd been doing? Offering a few moments pleasure as a substitute for crippling grief? She had no idea. Still, he'd wanted her. She knew that. She also knew he'd fought it.

There had been a desperate urgency to his lovemaking. It made her feel special—loved.

*Loved?* The word sent doubt slicing through her with its razor-sharp edge. Was his gift of lovemaking another service he provided? Just part of the job?

Suddenly his weight was oppressive, his breaths seared her flesh, and there was no trace of the tenderness with which he'd guided her to exquisite pleasure.

She pushed at his shoulder.

He carefully rolled off her and leaned against the burled wood headboard, holding out his arm in invitation.

Reluctantly, she let him pull her against his side.

His embrace tightened and he pressed a soft kiss to her temple. "How're you doing, Annie?"

*Scared, thank you.* "I'm fine," she lied. Zane McKinney had spoiled her for other men. She'd only known him for a couple of days. Yet he'd imprinted himself on her like a tattoo. This—the sex—was only part of it. He'd already won her heart with his integrity, his honor, his focused intensity.

How could she walk away now? How could she go back to her lonely life? Even if he was *just doing his job,* she'd been forever changed by his gentle touch and fierce tenderness.

ANNA WOKE WHEN ZANE turned over. She opened one sleepy eye. His lean buttocks and long powerful thighs flexed as he stood.

Sleek golden skin accented the muscles in his back and shoulders as he pulled on his slacks. A shiver of remembered pleasure tingled deep inside her as he reached for his shirt. The light filtering through the drapes planed his muscles in ripples of light and shadow.

She sat up. He turned, shrugging into his shirt.

The harsh line of his jaw was as sculpted as flint. His eyes were hooded and stormy. The unflappable Texas Ranger was back.

Anna raked her teeth over her bottom lip and bunched the sheet in her fist. *No.* The man standing before her was anything but unflappable. He was pissed.

"Zane? Is something wrong?"

He didn't answer. He quickly tucked his shirt into his slacks and zipped them. He raked a hand through his hair as he stuck his feet into his shoes.

"Where—are you going?"

"I need to get to work," he said flatly. "I've wasted too much time."

*Wasted.* The word hurt her. Stop it, she scolded herself. It was just sex. And she, too, needed something to do to fill her mind and keep her from dwelling on the pleasure he'd given her.

She bit her lip and met his gaze. "Are you

going to the police station? May I go with you? I don't really want to sit in this room by myself."

His expression darkened, and he opened his mouth. He was going to say no. Instead, he clamped his jaw and assessed her for an instant. With a seemingly careless shrug he walked around the bed and into the bathroom.

Anna jumped up and grabbed her jeans and a little blue T-shirt. She knew better than to make him wait.

ZANE STALKED across the short expanse of sidewalk that separated the Matheson Inn from the police station, moving just fast enough that Anna couldn't keep up. Which was his intention. He couldn't bear to look at her face and see her beautiful, pink-tinged cheeks and sparkling eyes. She glowed.

A few pairs of eyes followed them, darkening Zane's mood even more. Could they tell? To him, Annie looked like she'd just been well and thoroughly loved. Was it his imagination, or did others see it, as well?

And what about him? He'd barely glanced into the mirror in her bathroom as he'd washed up. He hadn't looked any different, but now his cheeks burned and it was all he could do to keep from smiling. Which irritated him even more.

The station door was locked, which meant there was no one inside. Quickly, automatically, he ticked off the deputies and their assignments. Burns and Enis had been at the funeral service and at the gravesite. He'd assigned Spinoza to watch Annie's room and car during the funeral, in case anyone tried to break in. The transcriptionist wasn't due back until the next day.

As he unlocked the door, Annie caught up to him. He could smell her evocative scent. Inside, he used another key to unlock Carley's office. He had to move Lou Ann and Justin Hendricks's case files from the side chair to give Annie a place to sit. He could only hope she hadn't noticed the labels.

"What are those?"

Zane winced. *Fat chance.* She was a reporter. Her job was to notice things. "File boxes."

"*'Hendricks. Unsolved.'* They're my mother's and Justin's case files, aren't they?"

There was no reason for him to answer.

"I want to see them."

"*Anna,* I have something I need to do. You can stay here, but I've got work to do."

His fingers itched to retrieve the note he'd

plucked off the bouquet of dead roses and read it. He couldn't believe he'd allowed himself to be distracted by her. What an idiot he was. Not only had his concern for her overridden his professional detachment, but he'd let it get out of hand.

What was it about her? He'd never felt so completely out of control, not even when he was a hormone-ridden teenager. Whatever had possessed him to give in to his desire, it had to stop—now. He had a murder to solve, and a woman, especially this woman, was not going to annihilate the focused detachment he'd spent years perfecting.

"Let me help."

He sighed and sent her a level glance. "No."

She stiffened and stuck her chin out. "I'm a good reporter. I have a stake in this. And I need *something to do*."

His gaze slid over her stubborn chin and vulnerable mouth. He cursed silently. Maybe it would keep her busy and out of his hair. She was way too much a distraction.

"I haven't had a chance to go through the boxes," he said resignedly. "Why don't you look at Justin's file?"

"Why don't I look at my mother's first?"

It was a waste of breath to expect that she'd

do what he said. "Listen to me, Anna. I know you've covered murders and rapes and traffic accidents. But this is *your mother.* I don't think you want to see the crime scene photos and the record of the autopsy."

Her mouth turned white at the corners. "I saw my sister. What do you suggest I do? Sit here and do my nails or read a fashion magazine? I need to help. I need to find out who did this." She eyed the boxes. "Everything's labeled, right? I'll just—" she swallowed "—avoid the graphic details."

He shoved Lou Ann's box toward her and stared at the tumble of golden-brown hair that fell across her face as she leaned over to take off the top.

His cell phone rang. It was Deputy Spinoza.

"What did you find out? Did you pick up the flowers?"

"Yes, sir. Mr. Warren, the owner of the florist shop, says that around here roses dry out in a couple of weeks. He says these dried out in the vase, because the heads have dropped."

"Okay. Good." Zane made a note on his PDA. "What about the purchase records?"

"He went back six months. That includes Valentine's Day. There were thirty-three purchases of red roses."

"And our short list?"

Zane heard paper rustling as Spinoza looked through his notes. "Valentine's Day— Leland Hendricks, Jim McKinney, and Rosa Ramirez purchased red roses. Other than that, Stella McKinney bought two dozen on March thirteenth—"

*Her birthday.*

"—and Hendricks made one other purchase, in April. McKinney bought a dozen roses in late May."

"What about Donna Hendricks?"

"No, sir. Not in the past six months."

"Find out who those purchases went to, then get your report written up and have Lottie transcribe it." Zane pocketed his cell phone and pulled out the note. He glanced at Anna, but she was bent over the box, inventorying the contents.

Using a pen and a letter opener, Zane spread the note open. As he reached for a plastic bag from his coat pocket, his eyes skimmed the printed letters.

Tell me what you know, Anna, or you will find dead roses on *your* grave.

The childlike printing was probably unidentifiable, but the message was all too clear.

A hand on his shoulder and a tiny gasp told him Anna was standing looking over his shoulder. She'd read the message.

"Where did you get that? From those roses on my mother's grave?"

He carefully slid the note into the plastic bag. "You saw them?"

"First thing, but I didn't see a note." She leaned down, her head almost touching his as she studied the note more closely. "It's dry."

He nodded, impressed, then immediately regretted it when his movement dislodged her hair, and it slid forward, skimming across his cheek.

His body betrayed him by springing to hard, hot life at the remembered feel of her silky hair floating over her naked shoulders as he'd brought her to climax with his thumbs.

He squeezed his eyes shut and pushed away from her. He picked up the bag. "And it rained last night, as we know. That means the killer left the note there this morning, before the funeral."

"He's arrogant."

"Or desperate." Zane stood and crossed his arms, glaring down at her.

"So, Anna, what does the killer want from you that's so important he's willing to risk exposure to find out? So important that he's willing to kill you to get it? And why is he so sure that you haven't already told me what it is?"

## Chapter Ten

Anna tried her best not to look guilty, but she failed. She knew it by the spark in Zane's eyes. He saw right through her and she hated that. How did he read her so easily? As soon as she asked herself that question, she knew how silly it was. The answer was obvious. Because he'd been in her bed. He'd been in *her.* And despite the fact that he wasn't her first lover, he'd coaxed from her what no other man ever had—he'd laid her open.

Anything he'd wanted to know had been right there. Her mind, her heart, as exposed as her body.

But it was over now, and if she knew him at all, he'd already sworn to himself that it would never happen again. He'd even stopped calling her Annie. Still, what gave him the right to be so sexy and so confident and so—so *right?*

She raked her upper teeth across her bottom lip and lifted her chin. "You want to know why he's sure I haven't told you? Because he's finally figured out that I don't know what Sarah knew—"

His gaze didn't waver, but he raised his brows.

She swallowed. "Yet."

Zane nodded once and pressed his lips together in a thin line. His accusing gaze grew sharp and hot as a predator's. "But you know where to find it."

Embarrassment burned her cheeks. Fear clutched at her insides. She had to tell him, but how could she? Her heart was torn in so many pieces. If Lou Ann had named her killer—Sarah's killer—then the evidence was in Lou Ann's suitcase. And as badly as Anna wanted to know who it was, as much as she wanted to put the tragedy behind her and get back to her safe lonely life, she was terrified of the answer.

She understood Zane's drive to get at the truth, but she also understood the shadow that sometimes haunted his smoky eyes. Funny thing—they were both afraid of the same thing.

*What if his father had murdered her mother and sister?*

Guilt flared up in her heart, not quite overwhelming the fear. "I should have told you—"

He sat up. "Damn right you should have. Annie, we already know this person is willing to hurt or to even kill to get hold of what Sarah knew."

"Do you have Sarah's suitcase?"

"Her suitcase?" His palm hit the desktop. "I should have known." He vaulted up out of the chair and crossed the room in two long strides and disappeared through the door.

Anna glanced down at her mother's evidence box. It was marked Unsolved. An ache of loneliness pulsed through her as she picked up the item on top—a makeup case. She smiled sadly and lay it aside. Several folders, some thick, some thin, were stacked on top of other bulky objects.

She rummaged around for a couple of seconds, then came up with a videocassette labeled *Evidence: Hendricks #4* and the date.

Just then Zane returned with her sister's old hard-sided suitcase. It was a dingy tan color, with brown leather trim. He set the case on the edge of the desk and thumbed the latches open. As he lifted the lid, Anna's eyes stung.

He stepped back and gestured for her to take over.

"Deputy Burns went through everything. So did I. I also examined the case itself closely."

She stood. "You ripped the lining."

"Of course."

She nodded. *Of course.* He'd been searching for clues, for evidence. She was surprised that he hadn't dismantled it, torn it off its hinges. If he had, he'd have found the false bottom.

"Come on, Anna. You asked for Sarah's suitcase. Here it is. What did I miss?"

She ran her fingers along the leather trim. "Actually, it was my mother's."

Zane's pulse sped up, despite his skepticism. He'd told her the truth. He'd gone over the damned case with the proverbial fine-toothed comb, and found nothing. Its exterior was too textured to yield a print, and the leather trim wasn't any better.

He should have taken it apart piece by piece.

He cursed himself silently. The only reason he hadn't was Anna's quiet, grief-stricken plea to get it back. He'd been suspicious of her reason for wanting it, but ultimately, she'd suckered him with those olive-green eyes. So he'd avoided tearing the case up looking for evidence.

"Your mother's," he said. "And somewhere in here is the key to her murder?" He laughed shortly. "You actually had me believing you wanted it to remember your sister by."

Anna's gaze shot to his. But almost before he registered the hurt that glistened in her eyes like tears, she'd turned her attention back to the brown case.

It was unremarkable, except for its age. It measured twenty inches by twenty-four, and thirteen inches deep. Two metal latches with spring locks kept it closed.

"See this scratch?" she asked. "Sarah and I were trying to put our cat inside it." Her mouth turned up in a little smile as she traced the jagged mar.

"And this?" She pointed at a pencil scribbling. "I remember wanting to write Las Vegas, but I was too little. I didn't know how to write. Mom used to point out all the stickers to us—Paris, New York—" She touched them. "I wanted my city to be on it, too."

"Anna, enough with the trip down memory lane." Zane felt mean, but this was a murder investigation, damn it. And it was fast spiraling out of his control.

She nodded, the movement dislodging a tear that carved a damp path down her cheek. "All right, Lieutenant. Watch closely."

Her slender fingers slid along the bottom inside edge of the case. Zane followed her every movement intently. At evenly spaced intervals were tiny brads. After a few seconds, Anna slid a fingernail under a brad and lifted. He heard a barely discernible click. Then she slid her fingers farther along, stopped and lifted another brad, then a second or two later, a third.

He watched in fascination as the bottom of the case popped up by a fraction of an inch. Fishing out his pocketknife, he slid the point under the edge, gaining enough traction to pry the piece of fabric-covered cardboard up.

"A false bottom," he muttered. And not a clunky deep one that would be obvious on close examination. This space was barely deep enough to hide a couple of sheets of paper. And that's exactly what it did. "I'll be damned. Where did Sarah get this suitcase?"

"I told you. It was my mother's. A magician she dated for a while gave it to her."

That explained it.

Anna made a sound—barely audible yet filled with grief. Zane knew how she felt. Whatever Sarah had known about her mother's killer was right in front of them.

His fingers itched to grab the paper, but that ridiculously unprofessional part of him—the part that empathized with Anna's conflicting feelings—held back. The slip of paper was evidence, but it was also the only thing she had of her mother and sister.

Anna reached for it, then paused and glanced at him, a question in her gaze.

He nodded slightly, berating himself for a sentimental fool.

She picked it up. The cream-colored sheet fluttered in her unsteady hand.

His entire body screamed with impatience as she bit her lip and blinked several times. Her other hand went to her mouth, muffling a small sob.

Just when Zane thought he couldn't wait another second, she spoke.

"It's a note to me," she said, her voice choked with strain. She raised her head and met his gaze. "On Matheson Inn stationery."

"What?" Zane stood and looked over her shoulder.

"She wrote this while she was waiting for me." She took a deep shaky breath.

"'Anna-banana, I'm so sorry I left you. I hope you can forgive me. I want us to get past Mom's death and be a family. We can drink a toast—a non-alcoholic toast—to new beginnings.'"

Anna's voice gave out and she sank back down onto the chair. She dropped the paper to her lap and pressed both fists against her mouth. Her shoulders shook.

Zane gingerly picked up the piece of paper and read the last three lines to himself.

"'But just in case, I want you to remember one thing. Never forget what Mom always said about secrets.'"

"'Hey, Anna-banana, I'm so sorry I left you. I hope you can forgive me.'"

He couldn't contain his sigh of mixed relief and frustration. He was so afraid he'd see his father's name written in Sarah's neat rounded hand. If he had…well, it would have proven that his suspicions, his fears, were right.

But the note didn't implicate anyone. For the first time, he believed that Anna really didn't know anything. Not a comforting thought since he'd been pinning his hopes of wrapping up this case on the secret he'd known she was hiding.

He stepped over to the desk and pulled out a clear plastic evidence bag and slid the single sheet of paper into it. No sense in taking any chances. The paper might have trace evidence on it.

Then he turned to the suitcase. His gaze met Anna's.

"Sorry," he said as he lifted the piece of covered cardboard that formed the false bottom and ripped it out.

Retrieving his pocketknife, he slit the board then broke it in two. Nothing. He peeled the fabric from the cardboard. Still nothing.

He examined the tear where he'd ripped the board out. Nothing there, either.

Behind him, he heard Anna's sobs. Her grief called to him. He wanted desperately to pull her into his arms and comfort her. But he couldn't. He'd already wasted too much time on useless, reckless self-indulgence. If a Ranger under his charge had done the things he'd done, he'd bring them up on *Conduct Unbecoming*.

*No more.*

From now on, he was Lieutenant McKinney, chief investigator on this case, and Anna was nothing more than his prime witness.

"Okay," he said crisply, ignoring the little jerk that told him he'd startled her out of her grief-soaked haze. "Explain the note to me. What's this about secrets?"

Zane's voice buzzed in Anna's ears. She tried to pull herself back into the present, but it was a long way up from her valley of grief and loss.

Then his warm strong hand gripped her shoulder gently, and gave it a reassuring squeeze. "Annie?"

She straightened her back and wiped her fingers across her damp cheeks.

"I'm sorry. What did you say?" Tears were still there, lurking close to the surface, but she compressed her lips and managed to deter them, at least for a while.

"I asked what Sarah was referring to when she mentioned secrets."

*Secrets?* "I don't know. We used to play a game called Secrets but it was just a child's game, kind of like Gossip."

"Think, Annie. Are you sure there's nothing else? If Sarah told you she had proof that would convict your mother's killer, where is it?" His impatience and frustration were palpable. It thrummed between them just like their dangerous attraction to each other.

"I don't know!"

"Could she have witnessed the killing? Could her proof be her eyewitness account of the murder?"

"No! If she'd seen the person who killed our mother, she'd have testified back then."

"Not if she was scared. Maybe the killer knew she'd seen him."

Anna shook her head. What Zane was suggesting was worse than anything she'd imagined. "If she'd known who the killer was, why would she have left me here alone?"

Zane's eyes went from stormy to soft heather-blue. "I'm sure she wouldn't have," he said. "But where's the proof? That note, that reference to your mother's secrets, is a clue. What did your mother say about secrets?"

Anna clasped her hands together and swore to herself that she wouldn't break down. "I don't remember. All I can think of is—" she stopped and swallowed "—is Sarah in that room writing me a note."

She looked deeply into his eyes. "She

knew, didn't she? She knew someone was going to kill her."

His face was still, carefully blank, yet she could read his thoughts clearly. He thought Sarah had written the note out of guilt.

"You think she told me she had proof just to get me to meet her here so she could tell me about her baby. But you're wrong. She knew there was a chance she'd run into the killer if she came here."

"So she hid the proof somewhere. We've taken that room apart. So where is it?"

"What about her car? What about somewhere else in the hotel?"

"I'll reinterview the desk clerk. Make sure we know every step she took that evening."

Anna nodded. "And I'll try to figure out what Sarah's note means." She looked down at the evidence box. "Maybe if I go through all this, it'll trigger a memory."

She picked up the videocassette.

"What's that?" He took it from her.

"It was in Lou Ann's box."

"An evidence tape," he muttered as he read the label.

Just then the desk phone rang. Zane picked up the handset. "McKinney."

Anna watched his face. She didn't even pretend not to listen.

He nodded. "Yeah, Sloan, I'm okay, and no I haven't gone by the parents' house." He paused.

"Good. It's about time you got your butt over here. Why wait? Why not tomorrow, or better yet, tonight?" He flopped into the desk chair and raked his fingers through his hair.

"Well, fine, big shot. You have your meeting with the commissioner. Then maybe you could start wandering over this way." He started to press the disconnect button, but Sloan obviously said something.

"No," he snapped. "I haven't. He doesn't have a credible alibi, and Mom's about to lose it. She defends him one minute and acts like she knows he's guilty the next. Well, come on down. Maybe you can sort it all out."

He slammed the handset back onto its base and sucked in a deep breath.

Anna saw his grief and worry etched in the faint lines around his eyes and the pinched corners of his mouth. He wiped his face with one hand and erased the emotion.

"Zane, do you want to watch the video-tape?"

He leveled a scathing gaze at her. "I'll be going through the entire contents of the box." Glancing at his watch, he stood.

"It's late. After eight. You need to get back

to your room. I'll walk you over there. We can run by the diner first if you want to pick up something to eat."

So he was dismissing her. The thought of going back to her room, where her bedclothes lay wrinkled and tangled and the decorative pillows were tossed haphazardly onto the floor, filled her with apprehension.

She didn't want to have to see the reminders of their lovemaking. She didn't want to get into that bed where the masculine woodsy scent of him clung to the sheets. An aching sense of regret washed through her.

As much to test his response as to distract herself, she said, "You mean, you're not going to make me sleep with the vending machines?" She punctuated the com-ment with a little smile.

"You'll be fine." His glare softened slightly. "Are you afraid the killer can get to you?"

Anna wasn't afraid of the killer right this minute. She was afraid of her own thoughts. She was afraid of being alone in that hotel room where they'd made love.

"Where are you going to sl—be?"

He gestured toward the evidence boxes. "I still have a lot of work to do. I'm probably going to be here most of the night."

"Can I stay with you? I mean—I won't bother you."

Irritation flared in his eyes but it faded quickly. He blinked. "Sure."

His answer surprised her. She'd been certain he'd refuse. Was *he* worried that the killer might try to get to her again? That thought was not comforting.

"I'd like to watch the tape with you."

He opened his mouth, but before he could say no, she plunged ahead. "You said I could look at my mother's evidence."

After a brief pause, Zane stood. "Okay, but you better prepare yourself. We don't know what this is. It could be a videotape of the crime scene."

In other words, she might see her mother dead, just like Sarah. Bitter trepidation tightened her throat. "I know."

He pushed back from the desk and stood. "I'm going to get something cold to drink. Want anything?"

"Water, or maybe a diet cola. Didn't I see some crackers in one of the machines?"

He nodded and left the room.

With him gone, she pushed out breath in a huge sigh, and felt the tears coming back. She squeezed her eyes shut and lectured herself.

Crying didn't accomplish anything, except make her feel bad and ruin her makeup, on the rare occasions she wore it. Crying sucked away energy and left her exhausted.

Wiping angrily at the wet trails on her cheeks, she picked up the tape. Getting it set up would distract her. She looked around. A small TV sat on top of a file cabinet. She stood up and examined it. It was a combined TV and VHS recorder/player. Sitting beside it was a remote control.

She turned on the TV, inserted the tape and pressed Play. The image that appeared on the screen was familiar. She'd lived in that huge house for over two years. She was looking at Leland Hendricks's security tapes.

The date stamp in the lower right corner of the screen told her this tape was made the day Lou Ann was killed. The time stamp read 4:00 p.m.

"Hendricks probably had tapes running twenty-four hours a day."

Anna jumped. She hadn't heard Zane return. He handed her a diet cola and two bags of chips. He set a grape soda and several snack bags on the desk then sat down in the desk chair and turned it toward the TV.

Anna popped the top on her cola and sipped at it, eyeing his drink. "Grape soda?"

His gaze snapped to hers and a smile curved his lips. He shrugged one shoulder. "Old habit. Gotta have my sugar fix." He turned back to the TV screen. "He must have had them set up to start every eight hours—4:00 p.m., midnight and 8:00 a.m. These days it's a lot easier with DVD technology."

They watched in silence for a few minutes, but nothing changed on the screen, except for leaves rustling on the trees and an occasional bird or insect flying by.

"I remember Leland was incensed that he had to account for his whereabouts at the time of the murder." Anna shook her head as she watched a cat slink across Leland's driveway. "He finally offered the sheriff this security tape as proof that he never left the house."

"Where were you and Sarah that night?"

His question magnified the heavy sense of trepidation that blanketed her whenever she thought about that night and the days that followed. "I was spending the night with a friend. Mom suggested it. Sherri was my best friend." Sudden realization dawned, surprising her. "Mom did that on purpose. She wanted me out of the house!"

"Could be. Any idea why? Were she and Leland having problems?"

"Mom's only problem with Leland was Justin. She didn't like having him living with us. Said she'd done her time changing diapers and chasing a toddler around."

Zane pulled out his PDA and made a note. "What about Sarah?"

"Sarah had a new boyfriend. She was never home."

"And Justin and his sister? Where were they?"

"I think Rosa was baby-sitting them. I went home with Sherri from school, so the first I knew of what had happened to Lou Ann was when the sheriff showed up. I remember thinking if I'd been home, maybe I could somehow have saved her."

Zane held out his hand for the remote. She gave it to him, doing her best to avoid touching his hand. But he brushed her fingers with his. "I'm sorry, Annie."

She nodded.

He fast-forwarded to a few minutes after six.

"There's his car, pulling in," Anna said.

"He doesn't live that far from the Matheson Inn. Why did the sheriff accept this tape as his alibi? He could have gone out the back and walked to the inn."

She stood and pointed to the left side of

the screen. "There's no door on the back of the house. There's one leading into the house from the garage, the front door, of course, and this one. You can barely see it from this angle, but it exits from the kitchen, which is right behind the garage. No matter which way he left, the camera would have picked him up."

"Hold it. What's going on?"

Anna saw it almost as soon as Zane did. The date/time stamp disappeared from the edge of the screen.

He rewound the tape for a few seconds, then played it again. Anna watched closely.

"There," she said. "Right at 6:08 p.m. the time stamp goes off, but I didn't see anything change on the screen. There must have been a defect in the camera."

"Hmm." Zane didn't sound convinced. He let the tape play. The date and time reappeared at 6:14 p.m.

"Six minutes. That jibes with my watch. So there's no time missing." He pressed fast-forward again. "What was the exact time of the murder?"

"I'm not sure." She felt like an observer, watching Zane and herself discussing her mother's murder as if it were just another tragic story to be reported. It was an odd feeling, sad, and yet comforting. Unlike the queasy, helpless sense of loss she'd lived with for the past sixteen years.

Maybe working together, she and Zane could finally find the killer, and bring closure—for a lot of people.

"Look in the box. Find the medical examiner's report."

She rummaged among the folders until she found one labeled M.E. She opened the folder and found a form labeled Death Certificate that had been filled in by a steady hand. "Here it is. Time of death—between 9:15 p.m. and 9:22 p.m."

Zane stopped the tape at 8:53 p.m. "Okay, we're at twenty-two minutes before your mother was killed."

They sat there together, watching the unchanging picture on the screen. Leland had lawn lights, so it would be easy to see any movement. At 9:12 p.m., the stamp flickered off.

Anna glanced at Zane, who checked his watch. The next few minutes seemed interminable. But finally, the stamp flickered back on.

"Nine-eighteen." She studied the image on the screen. "Nothing happened. So I guess Leland's alibi holds up."

Zane rubbed his cheek and chin, then checked his watch.

There was something he didn't like about what he'd seen. "What is it?"

He shook his head, his mouth set, a tiny furrow etched between his brows. "Did that seem like six minutes to you?"

She shrugged. "I don't know. Maybe the short in the camera, or whatever it is, is random. We should test several other places."

He nodded, never taking his eye off the screen. "Right. We should. Let's make sure we do this accurately." He handed her the remote. "Rewind and run that section again, and mark out loud when the stamp disappears and when it reappears. I'll time it on my watch."

Anna rewound the tape to 8:56 p.m. and pressed Play. Both of them sat unmoving as the timer crept forward, minute by minute. Finally the stamp read 9:11 p.m.

"Okay, get ready," she whispered.

Zane slipped his watch off his wrist and held it up, in line with his view of the screen.

The one changed to a two.

"Mark," she said, her pulse speeding up. She kept her eyes on the screen, searching for anything out of the ordinary—a slight movement, a shadow, anything that could be Leland sneaking out of his house.

At 9:14 p.m., the picture wavered.

Anna's heart thumped in her chest. Her finger went automatically to the Pause button. She had to stop herself from pressing it. This was about time elapsed. Not a slight waver that could have been caused by a dirty machine or a worn-out tape.

But her pulse still hammered. She stared unblinking at the screen, in case anything else looked odd. Finally the numbers flipped to 9:18 p.m. "Mark!"

Zane scooted closer to her, the rollers on his chair rumbling loudly on the hardwood floor. "Take a look." He held out his watch.

He'd used a stopwatch function. The time read exactly five minutes.

"I was right," Zane said. "I'm going to send this tape to the media lab and let them test the whole thing. They're much better equipped to determine if the timing is random or not."

He started to get up to retrieve the tape from the recorder, but Anna caught his forearm. Her fingers were warm.

"Zane, wait. I want you to see something."

He looked down at her hand. It was small and pale next to his sun-browned skin. Her fingernails were short and neatly rounded. No polish. And no rings.

The sound of the tape rewinding pulled him back into the moment. "See what?"

She stopped the tape, then pressed Play.

"Right here—coming up." Her fingers tightened on his arm. "There! Did you see it?"

"No." He cursed silently. He'd been too busy considering all the differences between men and women, specifically the differences between Anna and him. Like that pale beautiful skin. Like her firm supple breasts and the way she'd moaned when he'd touched her.

*Damn it!* He shifted just enough to slip his arm out from under her hand. Her touch was too distracting.

"What am I supposed to see?" he said shortly.

He felt her stiffen. "Just watch it, please. I want you to see it for yourself."

"Okay." He concentrated on the image. Absolutely nothing happened, 9:12 p.m. had been on the screen for about twenty-five or thirty seconds. Then something changed.

He blinked. "What was that?"

"Watch it again."

He did. "The picture sort of wavers. It happens at the same place every time."

"Yes."

Her voice was lilting, excited. This must be what she was like when she was working, reporting on a story. He stole a glance. Her eyes sparkled, her cheeks were pink. She was so fresh and lovely she made him ache with want just to look at her.

"I've seen insurance fraud cases and divorce investigations where videotapes were altered. This reminds me of how those tapes looked. I've seen experts show the tape frame by frame."

Zane felt stunned—speechless with the implication. His brain raced. His heart thudded in his chest. He flopped heavily down into the desk chair.

"What do you think?"

Her excitement was palpable, but right at the moment, Zane couldn't think past his own emotions.

"You're saying Leland tampered with the tape?" He heard the breathless tension in his voice.

"I think so. There could be a whole minute missing. That's plenty of time to get out of the house and away from camera range. If he left at nine-twelve, could he get to the inn, kill my mother, and get back home before the sheriff contacted him with the news that his wife was dead?"

*Could he?* "With a little planning and a lot of luck."

Zane couldn't sit there any longer. He stood and walked out of the sheriff's office and down the hall to the break room. The room was dark except for the red and blue vending machine lights. He paced back and forth, rubbing his neck, his face, doing his best to think rationally, like a Texas Ranger.

He'd spent sixteen years weighted down by the guilt of his father. His entire career as a Ranger had been based on his will, his drive to prove to the Rangers and to himself, that he was nothing like Jim McKinney. That he was trustworthy, honorable. That he was Ranger material. It had been hell, seeing the looks on his fellow Rangers' faces, hearing their muttered comments, enduring their disdain.

Now, with one flicker on a TV screen, everything had changed.

Zane had been—hell, the whole town, the whole state of Texas, had been convinced that Jim McKinney was guilty. Except for a technicality and a good lawyer, Jim would be serving time for murder. He was the only suspect who had the trifecta—motive, means and no alibi.

But if Leland Hendricks had tampered

with his security tape, then the case against McKinney fell apart.

Zane massaged the knot at the back of his neck as his thoughts raced, ticking off the pieces of evidence against Leland.

He had a stronger motive—several motives in fact. His wife was cheating on him, he needed money, and he'd taken out a substantial insurance policy on her life. He had means. He'd worked at the Matheson Inn. He probably knew every door and closet and back entrance in the building. It would have been a snap for him to sneak in the back door and slip up to her room.

And now, it was almost certain that his alibi was destroyed.

Leland Hendricks could have murdered his wife.

## Chapter Eleven

"Zane? Is something wrong?"

Of course she'd come looking for him. He should have followed his first impulse and walked outside. But if she'd found all the rooms empty, she'd be scared.

Hell, maybe he'd wanted her to follow him. He blinked, realizing his eyes were blurry with tears. What a sap he was.

"Just thirsty," he said tightly, hoarsely, reaching into his pocket for change.

"You didn't finish your grape soda." Anna frowned. Zane was obviously upset. She saw it in the tense curve of his back, heard it in his tightly controlled voice.

What had happened that would cause him to beso distressed? All they'd done was blow Leland Hendricks's alibi. It was a huge break in his case. Why wasn't he happy to have another suspect with no alibi other than his father?

*His father.*

"Zane?" The chink of coins hitting the cash box inside the drink machine echoed in the silence. "Whatever it is, I can help."

The can tumbled into the tray with a thunk. He grabbed it, still with his back to her. "It's after ten. If you're still planning to sleep here, you know where the blankets are." He gestured halfheartedly toward the closet. "I've got to get to work."

"This is about your father isn't it? I've seen the tension between you two. I know it must have been hard for you, with everyone believing he was guilty."

He shook his head and sat on the arm of the couch. He set the unopened can on the side table. He propped his elbows on his knees and stared at his hands.

After a moment he spoke. "Texas Rangers aren't just law enforcement officers," he said. "We're the peacekeepers, the heroes of Texas. Only the best make the cut. The code of the Ranger is never violated. We're held to a higher standard, and we always exceed it."

There was pride in his voice. But there was also something else. Maybe irony.

"But your dad violated the code."

He angled his head to look at her and she saw the shimmer of dampness in his eyes.

"He was the biggest, bravest man I ever knew. He was everything I wanted to be. I was older, but it was my brother Sloan who always knew what Dad really was—how he cheated on Mom." He laughed, a short, sharp sound. "I was too blinded by hero worship."

"You were sure he was guilty, but now, with Leland's alibi broken—"

"I spent sixteen years fighting to prove I was nothing like him. Sixteen years blaming him and your mother for wrecking my family, for ruining our lives."

Anna's throat tightened with emotion. She'd done the same thing. All the hurt, all the disappointment, all the grief he was feeling was familiar to her.

She longed to go to him, to cradle his head against her breast and comfort him. But she had no idea how he'd react. If he rebuffed her, it would break her heart.

So she used what she had—words. "Your father had a lot to atone for. So did my mother. You weren't totally wrong. They hurt a lot of people."

"You don't get it." He stood and walked over to the doorway. His back was still to her. "My career, my accomplishments.

Everything I've always been so proud of." He rubbed the back of his neck. "I've been fooling myself and everybody else. I didn't become a Ranger because I was dedicated to the cause. I didn't get to be lieutenant because I was honorable and brave and valiant. I got to where I am today because I wanted to rub my dad's nose in it." His voice was raspy with pain.

Anna knew he'd never spoken those words to anyone. It had probably never occurred to him until he'd returned to Justice.

She couldn't just stand here and let him hurt alone. So she stepped up close behind him and flattened her palms against his back. "I don't believe that."

"Believe it."

"I understand how you feel. I spent a lot of years blaming them for wrecking my life. But I finally had to convince myself that what they'd done didn't have to affect my whole life." She curled her fingers against the crisp cotton of his shirt.

"You were what—eighteen?—when my mother was murdered. Hardly more than a kid. You probably did want to rub his nose in your accomplishments then. But that's not how you feel now, is it?"

He turned and grabbed her hands. He

placed them against his chest. "Isn't it? Tell me, what do you see when you look at me?"

She stared up into his smoky eyes and knew she couldn't tell him the truth. That she saw the strongest, yet gentlest man she'd ever known, a hero and a lover. She saw the man who had spoiled her for any other man she might meet. She saw the man she loved.

She swallowed. "I see a brave, honorable man. And I see a boy whose father let him down." She pressed her palms more firmly against his chest. "And I feel a strong, generous heart beating inside that man."

His gaze turned soft and a ghost of a smile lightened his face. He let go of her hands and slid his palms along her forearms. "You're prejudiced. You only see what you want to see."

She caught her lower lip between her teeth, willing herself to back away, to stop this before he did. But she couldn't. Something inside her was driving her, something that flared like an oil lamp in a breeze. That something sent longing swirling through her. Longing and desire.

"And you?" she whispered. "What do you see when you look at me? That mousy freshman with the braces and the stringy hair?"

His hands cupped her elbows, then slid up her arms to her shoulders, then her neck. "I see a beautiful, intelligent woman who has a brilliant career and who will one day be famous—maybe even win a Pulitzer."

She laughed. "Oh, please! Why all the flattery?"

He bent his head until his forehead rested against hers. "Not flattery. Honesty."

He was too close for her to focus on his eyes. But his breath warmed her mouth and his fingers tilted her chin up.

"Zane—I thought you said this wouldn't happen again."

He nodded, rolling his forehead against hers. "I did. Stop me." His voice was husky.

"I don't think I can."

One hand slid down her back to cup her bottom. He pulled her closer, until his hard arousal pressed insistently against her.

Sweet, sharp thrills arrowed through her, all the way to the center of her desire. She moaned and pressed her lips to his neck, the soft, vulnerable skin beneath his jaw. His pulse beat rapidly, strongly. His arousal grew.

Lowering his head, he captured her lips. His kiss was different from any kiss she'd ever experienced. He moved slowly, drawing out the pleasure, making love to her mouth with his lips and tongue.

She parted her lips, giving him full access, inviting him in and kissing him back. Their tongues met and played, thrusting and exploring.

She felt boneless, as if she would collapse without his hands cupping her bottom and his mouth on hers. Her arms slid up to wrap around his neck.

Suddenly she found herself being lifted. He carried her to the couch and laid her down, then slid above her.

They melded together like two perfect parts of one whole. His arousal pulsed against her upper thigh, his chest heaved with his quick breaths, telling her how much he wanted her.

Then he lifted himself and looked deeply into her eyes. His were a soft heather-blue—not smoky with irritation or sharp with anger now.

"Annie, I'm here to work a case, not take advantage of my primary witness." Storm clouds began to form in his eyes.

"Take advantage?" She laughed dreamily. "Is that what you're doing? And here I thought you couldn't resist me. That maybe I was taking advantage of you." She ran her palms along the hard planes of his biceps, then caressed his chest as she arched slightly against him.

"Ah—" he rasped. "Maybe you are."

Then he kissed her again and all rational thought flew out of her head. Somehow, within seconds, their clothes were gone and they lay flesh to flesh.

His elegant hands traced her entire body, from her nose and chin to her collarbone and down, to cup and tease each breast, to palm her flat stomach and trace the swell of her hipbones. Then farther, caressing the delicate skin of her inner thighs.

His caresses moved closer and closer to her center. Finally, as she was about to scream with anticipation and longing, his palm pressed against her mound. His fingers probed, rubbed, teased, urging a response from her.

She floated on a sensual plane, far above the real world. Nothing existed but the magic touch of his fingers, the warmth of his mouth, the exquisite sensation of his hot bare skin against hers.

Just when she was about to reach the pinnacle, he stopped. "Touch me," he whispered, his voice ragged with passion. "Put your hand on me."

She complied, almost delirious with the feel of him, hard and smooth and pulsing against her palm. Then he slipped his finger into her and she lost the ability to breathe.

With her guidance, he slid into her, slowly but insistently. His face was alight with passion as he thrust again and again.

Anna shifted and met his thrusts with her own, until the building climax spread through her whole body. Then it came—the pinnacle. She cried out and clung to him as he groaned and strained, wringing from her the last bit of exquisite pleasure.

He buried his head in the hollow between her shoulder and neck, his chest heaving, his arousal slowly waning. She languidly caressed his back and shoulder. She slipped her fingers through his hair as she breathed in the woodsy masculine scent of him.

*How she loved him.*

Her drowsy brain roused in faint alarm and tried to analyze that thought, but it didn't get very far. She fell asleep.

A LOUD BANGING woke her. Anna squeezed her eyes shut and did her best to hold on to the delicious dream, reveling in the solid, smooth warmth that enveloped her.

But the banging continued. She shivered

as the warm masculine body peeled away from hers.

She opened her eyes. *Zane.* His magnificent buttocks and thighs flexed as he pulled his jeans up.

Zane glanced over his shoulder as Annie turned onto her side. The enticing curve of her hip and the delicate shadow between her legs brought life back to his spent body. He frowned and dragged his gaze away.

"Annie, get up," he snapped as he reached for his shirt. "There's somebody at the door."

He ran his fingers through his hair, double checked the buttons on his shirt, then zipped across the hall to the office where he grabbed his gun.

When he unlocked the front door, his gun hand behind him, his heart pounded in stunned reaction.

"Dad?" His voice sounded scratchy. He cleared his throat and frowned. "What are you doing here?"

Jim's blue gaze took in Zane's appearance with a wry smile. He gestured toward Zane's feet. "I guess you weren't expecting visitors."

Zane looked down. *Crap.* He was barefooted. He didn't even want to think what his hair looked like. Warmth spread across his neck and cheeks. "What do you want?"

Jim's smile faded at his tone. "I wanted to check on you—see when you're going to visit your mother."

Zane's hand tightened on the doorknob. "You came here this time of night to ask me that?"

"I just got off work. Doing inventory. After today I'm back on the three-to-eleven shift."

At a supermarket in the next town. A twinge of compassion pricked Zane's heart. Jim McKinney had been at the top of his game before Lou Ann was murdered. By now he might even be a captain. Instead, he was bagging groceries and counting boxes of diapers.

Zane shook off the crippling emotions those thoughts brought up. "Well, I'm busy. Got a case to solve."

Jim nodded. "You doing research in there tonight?"

Anger effectively wiped away the compassion. "That is none of your business."

His dad looked past him. "Hello there, Miss Anna," he said.

With an exasperated sigh, Zane backed up, opening the door wider for his father to come in.

"Mr. McKinney, how are you?"

She'd put her clothes on and done something to her hair. It was twisted up with wisps and tendrils escaping everywhere. Her cheeks were pink where his beard had scratched her tender skin. She looked sexy and beautiful and—satisfied.

Jim stepped over and took her hand. He bent and kissed it.

Zane rolled his eyes, earning him a venomous glare from her.

"Is everything all right?" she asked, looking from Jim to Zane.

Jim nodded. Zane scowled. He didn't know what had brought his dad out this late, but he figured it wasn't just to ask him over for dinner.

"Anna," Jim said, still holding her hand. "Would you excuse us for a few minutes? I'd like to talk to my son."

Her brows twitched delicately and her gaze sharpened, but she nodded. "Of course. I'll make some coffee. Y'all come and have a cup when you're through talking."

Zane almost stopped her, almost begged her to stay. He didn't want to talk to his dad.

His insides were all twisted into knots. He couldn't have explained how he felt about his father right then. His epiphany of his reason for becoming a Ranger had stunned him, and he needed time to sort out his feelings.

"So—what's so all-fired important you've got to talk to me at ten-thirty at night?" he bit out as he stepped over to the rack beside the door and slipped his gun into its holster.

Behind him, he heard the unmistakable sound of change jingling. His pulse jumped. It was a sound he recognized from his childhood. His dad had always jingled change in his pockets. More times than not he'd fish it out and toss it to him and Sloan.

The blue eyes assessed him. "You've done well for yourself, Bud."

*Bud.* He winced at the endearment. He'd always been Bud and Sloan had been Squirt. He didn't want to be reminded of all these childhood memories—back when his dad was still his hero.

His muscles tightened into knots. There was no way he was about to get into an "old times" talk with Jim McKinney. He wasn't ready for that.

"Lieutenant with the Texas Rangers," his dad said. "You can't get much better than that."

"You should know."

Jim sighed. "Son, I know I let you down. I let everybody down. Your mother, Sloan.

But especially you. I'm proud as heck of both of my boys—"

"Don't you mean all three of your boys?" Zane snapped. He knew he was being mean, but he had the awful feeling that if he let his dad get to him, he'd sit down and bawl like a baby.

"All three." Jim wiped his face with an unsteady hand. "I never claimed to be a saint. I'm amazed and proud that you all became Texas Rangers. But you're my first-born. I always knew you were Ranger material. I told your mother that the first time I saw you when you were about fifteen minutes old."

"Dad—" Zane's throat was too tight to talk. He swallowed. "Dad, why did you come here?"

"I wanted to tell you something."

He grimaced as apprehension arrowed through his chest. Was Jim about to confess? He felt ripped in two, his professional side warring with his personal side.

He'd just discovered evidence that implicated Leland Hendricks. He'd just accepted the idea that his father might not be guilty.

*Don't,* he begged silently, even as he drew on his training to detach himself. He crossed his arms. "Let's hear it then."

Jim took a deep breath. "I haven't been the kind of father I should have been. And Lord knows I've let Stella down. But, son, I didn't kill Sarah Wallace. You need to stop letting your hate for me influence the way you conduct this case."

The anger and hurt inside him built until it choked off his breath and burned his scalp. *Was he?* He had the awful feeling that it wasn't hatred that was skewing his focus. It was the opposite of hate. He was terrified that his father was guilty.

Jim glanced at his watch. "I'd better get home." He sent Zane a pleading look. "Son, check on your mother. She's not well."

"Not well? What's wrong with her?"

"Nothing physical. She's always been delicate emotionally. I'm afraid she may be falling apart—having a nervous breakdown, whatever they call it—"

The harsh ring of the office phone interrupted him.

Zane reached over the receptionist counter and grabbed the handset. "McKinney."

"Help me! Somebody hurt Richie!"

His heart leaped. "Where?" he snapped.

"The inn. Please hurry!"

"Be right there." He hung up and stalked over to the rack and grabbed his holster.

"What is it?" Jim asked.

"Something's happened at the inn."

"I'm going with you."

Zane opened his mouth to say no but just then Anna came in.

"The coffee's ready. Are you—" She saw Zane putting on his holster. "What's happened?"

He shook his head. "No, Dad, you're not going with me. Go home. Annie, take this extra set of keys and lock the double dead bolt behind us." He walked over to her and put the keys in her hand. "And don't open the door to anyone but me."

She nodded, her face suddenly pale.

He brushed his thumb across her cheek. "Don't be scared. Nobody can get in with the dead bolts locked."

Then he threw open the door and headed for the inn, hearing his dad's boots crunching on the sidewalk behind him.

ANNA GRIMACED and set the mug down next to the coffeepot. She shouldn't have drunk two cups. Now she'd never sleep.

She walked to the front of the building and checked the dead bolt to make sure it was locked. It was, just like the last three times she'd checked. Still, just to be safe, she checked the back door, too—for the fourth time.

Then she stood in the hall, wondering what was happening at the inn and why it was taking so long. Her heart skittered.

*Great. The damn caffeine.* She glanced at her watch. Only two minutes had passed since the last time she'd looked. Which meant Zane had been gone twelve minutes.

Why did it feel like an hour?

Just to have something to do, she emptied and cleaned the coffeepot and washed several mugs that had obviously been sitting in the sink for days.

She'd heard Zane and Jim talking. And even from the break room, she could detect the hurt that neither one of them could keep out of their voice.

Her heart ached for Zane, who'd lost his hero, and for Jim, who was obviously just a shell of the man he'd been.

Maybe once all this was over, they could heal the rift and be a family again.

*Family.* The word echoed in her head. She'd never had much family, just her mom and her sister. If her mother had any relatives, she'd never mentioned them, just like she'd never mentioned their father.

Now Sarah was gone, and Anna had nobody. Tears sprang to her eyes as she dried her hands on a dish towel.

But she did have Lou Ann's and Sarah's personal effects. Suddenly she longed to hold something of her mother's, to be close to her sister's things.

She walked down the hall to the sheriff's office. There was her mother's box of case files and evidence. But where were Sarah's things?

*The evidence room.* She'd heard Zane talk about it, but she had no idea where it was. She fished the key ring Zane had given her from her pocket and looked at it. Sure enough, one of the keys was labeled ER.

A part of her brain knew that snooping in the evidence room was wrong—possibly even illegal. But her need to feel some connection with her sister, to give herself a chance to grieve and remember, overrode her caution.

She walked down the hall, ticking off the doors. The sheriff's office, of course. Another office shared by the deputies. The interrogation room, the break room and, in the back, the bathroom. There was a door across from the bathroom.

*The evidence room.*

Anna's heart pounded and her mouth grew dry. She'd done some slightly questionable things to get at a story—never broken the law—not quite. She might have bent it to a nearly impossible angle once or twice.

She pressed a hand to her chest for a few seconds to calm her racing heart, then slipped the key into the lock and turned it. The door opened.

She turned on the light. The room was lined with file cabinets and shelves. The shelves were nearly empty, a testament to how little crime occurred in Justice.

The one window, directly opposite the door, was boarded up. A clipboard hung on a nail beside the door. Anna read the entries. The last one, dated today, was her mother's suitcase. Zane McKinney had signed it out and back in.

Anna traced the bold slanted letters. He signed his name with confidence and a slight impatience. She smiled.

Turning around, she surveyed the room. The suitcase should be in plain sight. Her gaze swept the shelves. There it was. It sat on a low shelf, next to a paper bag with Sarah's name on it.

She stepped over and lifted the case, then

set it down on the floor and opened it. It was empty. Sarah's clothes and personal effects must be in the paper bag.

A noise startled her. She jerked, then vaulted up and out the door. If it were Zane coming back, she'd have to endure his wrath. She pulled the door almost closed behind her and glanced at the front door, listening. Nothing else happened. No keys jangling. No muted conversation. It was totally quiet.

Still, she had to hurry. She checked her watch. Eleven forty-six. They'd been gone sixteen minutes already.

Back inside the room, she looked over at the paper bag, but right now it was the suitcase that held her attention. Zane had stuck the ripped-out false bottom back inside the case.

Her fingers traced the trick brads that had released the false bottom as memories from her childhood enveloped her. She and Sarah, leaving notes for each other inside the case, hiding their diaries there.

And of course her mom leaving them little surprises. Each time they opened the case, they found something. Maybe a funny bookmark, maybe a few of the baubles that were always falling off her dance costumes, sometimes a little journal or drawing pad.

Anna's eyes filled with tears and her throat tightened. Lou Ann had been a good mother. She'd done the best she could for her daughters.

Something niggled at the edge of her brain. Something about the case and Sarah's note.

*Secrets just lead to more secrets.* Sarah had warned her to remember their mother's words.

She closed her eyes and fingered the brads, trying to put herself back in time, trying to remember.

Then it hit her. *Secrets.* Her hand flew to her mouth as excitement bubbled up from her chest. *The false bottom.* Of course. The false bottom wasn't the real treasure. It hid another compartment. And *that* was where they'd hidden their most important notes.

*How did it open?* She closed her eyes and felt around the edge of the case, trying to pretend that her fingers were a child's fingers, and trying to find something that seemed familiar. She touched each brad, counting, trying to remember how to release the latch.

Then she found it. There was one brad that was infinitesimally larger than the others and slightly textured, where the others were smooth.

She slid her fingernail under it and lifted,

but nothing happened. In her mind's eye she saw Lou Ann showing her how to get it open.

*Of course!* She twisted the brad half a turn to the left then two complete turns to the right.

A soft click told her she'd succeeded. What appeared to be the bottom of the case had popped up, no more than a quarter inch. She lifted it and gasped.

There, in a compartment that was barely larger than the first, lay dozens of sheets of paper. Without touching them, Anna knew they were her mother's.

*This* was the proof of who had killed Lou Ann and Sarah. Anna reached for a sheet that looked like a letter from Lou Ann, but she stopped herself.

It was evidence. Maybe enough evidence to convict her mother's and sister's murderer. She needed to leave it alone and to let Zane inspect it. As much as her fingers twitched to dig into the thin stack of papers and receipts and notes, she didn't want anything to compromise the chain of evidence. Her experience as a journalist had taught her that any question about who'd touched evidence or where it had been could get a case thrown out.

What she needed to do was to put the case back and get out of here. If Jim or anybody else came back with Zane, she sure didn't want them to know what she'd found. She'd tell Zane when they were alone. She winced, imagining his anger when he realized she'd touched the case.

She stuck it back on the shelf, turned out the lights and exited, locking the door.

As the sound of the lock clicking echoed in the silence, a load of tension lifted from her shoulders and her eyes filled with tears. Finally, after all these years, maybe her mother could rest in peace.

Sticking the keys in her pocket, Anna walked down the hall to the break room to wash her hands and grab a bottle of water. She didn't bother turning on the light. The red and blue glow from the vending machines reminded her of how safe and sexy she felt in Zane's arms.

She let cool water from the sink run on her wrists for several seconds, then splashed her face, soothing her burning eyes. As she dried her face and hands, she heard another soft bump.

*Zane.*

She tossed the hand towel down and rushed out the door, turning toward the front room.

She heard a rustling noise behind her.

Confused, she turned. A dark looming shadow filled her vision.

Before she could react, the shadow moved and pain exploded in her head.

## Chapter Twelve

"I know you have it!"

Anna woke to dizziness. She felt as though her head were tumbling down a hill. She couldn't focus, couldn't get her bearings.

"Where is it? Tell me or you'll die!" The guttural voice penetrated through the haze of confusion that obscured her vision. Someone's punishing hands squeezed her upper arms, shaking her, literally scrambling her brains.

She squinted, trying to see something—anything—that would explain what was happening.

All she saw was darkness. The figure looming over her was cloaked in black. Even his head was covered by a large hood that obscured his face. The blue and red lights from the vending machines barely lit the hall; in fact, they added to the shadows.

The attacker slammed the back of her head against the floor. "Talk!"

She tried. "I don't—know—what you're—"

The figure slammed her head against the floor again. "You know, don't you?"

Anna shook her head desperately. "No!" She knew she was fighting for her life—knew if she didn't succeed she'd suffer the same fate as Lou Ann and Sarah.

Her vision was blurred and her head pounded. Still, she pushed at the cloaked figure and tried to scream.

But he had the advantage. He shoved her onto her stomach and wrapped something around her neck. She struggled, tried to push herself up to her knees, but he was too strong.

The strap tightened. Anna gasped and arched backward as the stiff garrote bit into her neck.

"Last chance," the rasping voice warned. "What did she give you? Where's the proof?"

Anna groped behind her, frantically grasping for something to grab on to. She was becoming light-headed from lack of air.

Suddenly her fingers touched heavy fabric.

*The cloak.* Wrapping her fingers around the handful of material, she clutched it as her vision went black and her lungs screamed out for air.

Something rang—a harsh death knell that filled her ears. Anna felt consciousness fading away.

*Did death sound like a cell phone?*

ZANE STALKED BACK to the sheriff's office, a cold anger simmering inside him. The attack on the desk clerk was nothing but a half-hearted attempt at a mugging.

Richie had been pushed to the ground just outside the door to the inn. His palms were scraped and his ego was bruised, but that was all. Zane had called one of the deputies to take his statement.

As he approached the building, a movement on the back side of the office caught his eye. Clouds obscured the moon, so all Zane could see was a dark shape heading across the parking lot away from the station.

*Annie.* His heart seized. He'd left her in the station alone. Had someone tried to get in?

He ran up the steps, key in hand, and unlocked the door and shoved it open. The reception area was dark. Maybe she was asleep.

As soon as he thought it, he knew it wasn't true. Something was wrong.

"Annie!" he shouted. "Annie, where are you?"

The faint glow from the vending machines wasn't enough light to see anything. He flipped the switch by the door and took in the reception area with a single glance.

Then he saw the small, crumpled figure lying on the floor of the hall—unmoving. His heart slammed against his chest wall—the pain of it nearly knocking him down.

"Annie," he croaked. *Dear God, don't let her be dead.*

His hand shook as he drew his weapon. His heart told him to go to Annie, but his head reasoned that the person who'd done this might still be in the building.

He grabbed his cell phone with his other hand and flipped it open, taking a few precious seconds to locate Jon's number and call him.

He crept forward, leading with his weapon, but unable to take his eyes off Anna.

She was so still, and a small puddle of blood was collecting beneath her head. There was a strap of some kind wrapped around her neck.

"No, God!" He knelt and put his fingers against her throat. He felt a faint pulse and his chest and gut cramped in relief.

"Dr. Evans." Jon's voice came through the phone.

"Jon—"

"Zane? What is it? What's the matter?"

"Jon, it's Annie. The station." His throat closed up. His eyes burned with tears.

"Hang on. I'm coming." Jon hung up.

Zane rose and did what he had to do. He checked every inch of the station and found nothing. No sign that anyone except Anna had been there.

A quiet little moan caught his attention. His pulse quickened. She was coming to.

He quickly checked the back door, using his handkerchief to turn the knob, but it was dead-bolted, just like he'd left it.

Turning and holstering his gun in one motion, he rushed to her side and knelt.

She uttered a soft cry and tried to push herself up with one hand.

"Annie—"

She froze, then lifted her head. "Zane?" Her voice was small and fractured.

"Yeah, honey, it's me. Stay still. Jon's on his way."

"Help me sit up."

"Okay, honey, just a minute." He dialed another number on his cell phone. "Spinoza, I need you to check out the back of the station. Someone broke in and attacked Anna, and I want the whole place gone over."

"What am I looking for?"

"Footprints, anything that tells us who it was and how they got in and out. Check the ground around the bathroom window."

"I'll get right on it."

"And call Enis. Someone attacked the desk clerk at the inn. I believe it was a distraction. The real target was Anna. Burns is at the inn, wrapping things up with Richie. Get one of them on checking alibis, and one of you grill the desk clerk. He was so scared he was about to pass out on me. Maybe he's calmed down now."

After disconnecting with Spinoza and putting his phone away, he sat beside Anna on the floor.

She threw her arms around his neck, squeezing so tightly, so desperately, that he couldn't help but respond. He wrapped his arms around her and held her close.

"It's okay, Annie. It's okay," he whispered. He held her and reassured her until Jon arrived.

Jon was there within ten minutes. He sat

her at the break room table and pulled a chair up beside her. After retrieving bandages and alcohol pads from his bag, he checked the bleeding abrasion on the side of her head.

While Jon made sure she was all right, Zane gloved up and unwrapped the strap from her neck and stuck it into an evidence bag.

"Tell me what happened," he said as he unwrapped a swab and gently took a sample from the abrasion on her temple. It was a long shot that it would yield anything except her own blood, but he couldn't overlook any possible evidence.

She sat as she'd been sitting the first time he'd seen her. Her head was high, her neck and shoulders stiff. She had her hands clasped in her lap, and she looked stunned.

Jon shone a light in her eyes, felt her neck and told her to swallow, then he looked down her throat. He nodded, giving her permission to talk.

She put a hand to her throat. "I was in the break room and I heard something." Her gaze met Zane's. "I thought it was you."

The look in her eyes shocked him. Her expression was filled with trust and something he couldn't name but that frightened him and sent his heart soaring at the same time.

"So I rushed out into the hall and—" She stopped to swallow and clear her throat. "And he…hit me."

"How did he get in? Did you unlock the rear door for some reason?"

She shook her head, her eyes on her hands. "No! I didn't touch the rear door. I didn't—" Her voice was getting higher and tighter.

"Hey, hey, Annie. It's okay." He squeezed her shoulder. "Jon, how is she?"

The doctor put away his alcohol pads and bandages. "No real damage." He smiled at Annie. "You'll have new bruises on your neck to go with the old ones."

She shuddered.

"And that bump on your head is going to give you a headache. Take some ibuprofen or acetaminophen. If the pain gets worse, or you start feeling dizzy, call me."

"Thanks, Jon," Zane said.

Jon nodded and shot him a look. Zane had no doubt as to his meaning. *Get her out of town, to a safe place.* He nodded at the doctor.

He sat in the chair Jon had vacated. "Okay, Annie. Tell me what happened. Start at the beginning."

"When I ran out of the break room, something slammed into my head. I fell. I must have passed out for a few seconds." She put a hand to her bandaged head and squeezed her eyes shut for an instant.

"The next thing I knew I was on the floor and he was looming over me. He said, '*I know you have it*,' and '*What did Sarah give you?*' Then he said, '*Where is the proof? Tell me or you'll die.*'" She began to tremble.

It pained Zane to see her like this. He felt guilty—responsible. He'd left her here alone.

He took her hand and her fingers squeezed his. "Are you sure it was a man? Was he tall, short, bulky, thin?"

"I'm not sure of anything. Whoever it was wore a thick black cloak. A cloak with a hood. He looked like Death—black hood and no face."

"Was it the same person who attacked you outside the inn?"

"Maybe." She pulled her hand out of his grip and studied it. "I tried to grab the cloak. It was heavy—like wool."

Zane took her hand again, this time to examine it. His pulse leaped. "There are black fibers under your nails."

He jumped up. "Don't move." He ran to the office, grabbed the evidence box and hurried back.

"I'm going to take fingernail scrapings.

Maybe we can somehow trace the material. When did you grab his cloak? What happened next?" He scraped under her nails and placed the scrapings in a plastic bag as she talked.

"He pushed me over onto my stomach. My head was still groggy, and pounding with pain."

Zane nodded. The bandage on her temple was barely whiter than her face. He had the urge to lean over and kiss away the single tear that trickled down her cheek. But he couldn't. He was not her lover, he was the investigator in charge of this case.

"He had a strap of some kind. Maybe leather. He wrapped it around my neck and— and strangled me, saying he'd kill me."

"What about his voice?"

She shook her head. "Whoever it was growled. He or she was obviously disguising their voice. I don't know why. He was going to kill me anyway." She smiled a sad, ironic smile.

Zane couldn't shake the longing to take her in his arms and promise her he'd keep her safe. But how could he promise that? He'd left her alone for less than twenty minutes and she'd been attacked. He and she would be a lot better off if he'd just focus on his job.

"Why'd he stop?"

"What?" She frowned at him.

"Why did he stop strangling you? Why did he run away?"

"I don't know that, either. I couldn't breathe. I tried to struggle but with no air I had no strength. I did hear some kind of ringing. I thought it meant I was dying. Then suddenly, the attacker was gone and I guess I passed out."

"What did the ringing sound like?"

"That's what's so odd. It sounded like a cell phone."

Zane stared at her. "A cell phone? Are you sure?"

Anna nodded. "Why?"

His brain was racing. A cell phone could mean that someone had called the murderer— warned him that Zane was headed back to the station.

"On my way back here, I saw a dark figure behind the station house."

"You saw him? My attacker?"

"Yeah. I should have pursued him, but I was afraid something had happened to you."

Anna heard the frustration in Zane's voice. If he hadn't felt obligated to check on her, could he have caught the murderer?

She, too, was sorry he hadn't grabbed the

cloaked figure, but the idea that his first thought was for her broke though the dense fog of terror that enveloped her.

"The dead bolt is still locked on the rear door. He must have come in through the bathroom window. Didn't you hear anything?"

"There was something—like a quiet thud. I couldn't tell where it came from. Then I heard it again a few moments later, while I was in the break room." Anna winced inwardly. She'd left herself wide open for his next question. And she knew by the look in his eye what he was about to ask. She swallowed nervously. It hurt her throat.

Zane pushed his chair back and sat with his elbows resting on his knees. He looked up at her from under his brow. "Where were you when you heard the first thud?"

"Zane, I—" She stopped at the venomous look in his eye.

He nodded and stood. "Save it. I know you're a reporter. It makes sense that you'd be snooping."

"I am a *journalist*. And I was not snooping. Besides, you're not going to believe what I found!"

He folded his arms and stared down his nose at her. "What?" he barked.

"I found the papers."

Zane's gaze sharpened. "Papers?"

She nodded eagerly. "I'd forgotten. The magician's suitcase—Mom was right. *Secrets only hide more secrets.*"

"What are you talking about?"

"Sarah's suitcase has two hidden compartments, one below the other."

"Are you telling me you went into the evidence room? That you touched the suitcase?" His voice was cold—hard.

She didn't like this icy professional with his accusations and his sudden aloof demeanor. She needed the gentle protector who had made her believe everything was going to be all right.

His gaze bore into her.

"I found Lou Ann's papers. I found the proof."

His mouth tightened into a straight line. "You found the *proof?* Damn it, Annie, do you have any idea what you've done? You've tampered with evidence. You could be accused of planting whatever is in that case."

"No. They're authentic. You'll see. They're my mother's. She kept receipts, notes—who knows what-all might be in there." Anna wanted to cry. She knew he'd be angry, but she hadn't expected this chilling, unforgiving calm. He acted like he'd been waiting for her to screw up his case.

Had he used her, taking the opportunity to leave her alone with the keys, figuring if Sarah had brought the proof to Justice with her, Anna would find it and his job would be done?

"It doesn't matter if there's a *signed confession* in there. You've compromised the evidence, broken the chain of custody. Do you understand?"

She nodded, biting her lip.

"What all did you touch?" he said on a sigh.

She lowered her gaze. She couldn't stand to see the anger and disappointment etched on his face. "After you and your dad left, I was thinking about you two, which led me to think about my mom and my sister. I missed them. I wanted to feel like they were nearby. It made sense that Mom's suitcase was in the evidence room. I took it off the shelf and just looked at it, thinking about when Sarah and I were children and we would hide notes and diaries in the case. Then I remembered what Sarah wrote. She warned me to remember what Mom always said about secrets."

She reached up to rub her temple and

winced when she encountered the bandage. "There's a second compartment. It's hidden underneath the first. It opens much like the first one did, with a certain sequence of brads."

Zane headed toward the door. "I'm going to check it out. Why don't you lie down?"

Anna opened her mouth to tell him she was too keyed up to relax, but he was already out the door and headed down the hall, his boots loud as his heels hit the hardwood floor.

*That was the sound!*

"Zane!" She sprung up out of the chair and stopped, her head spinning. She grabbed the chair back and waited for the dizziness to pass. Then, taking a deep breath, she headed down the hall to the evidence room.

"Zane—" She turned the corner and found him standing at a rolling table with the suitcase open before him, studying the contents.

He didn't look up. "I told you to lie down."

"Zane, the noise—the thud I heard? It was a boot, hitting the hardwood floor. The sound was exactly the same as the sound of you walking down the hall, only much quieter, as if the person was trying to be quiet."

He nodded shortly. "What did you touch?"

"In the suitcase? I opened the lid and

touched the brads. Then I lifted both false bottoms."

"Tell me how to get into the second false bottom."

She ran through the sequence, watching him as he performed each step perfectly. Finally, the inner hidden layer was exposed.

Zane stared at the contents of the second false bottom. "Did you handle anything?"

"Inside the flap? No."

He looked at her from underneath his brows. "What about the papers?"

"I didn't touch them. I swear. I saw what they were, and I knew it would cause problems if I touched them."

"You knew Sarah had put this information here."

"I knew she'd probably used the false bottom, but I'd forgotten about the second compartment." Anna's head was swimming again. She leaned against the door facing. "What do you see? I thought I saw receipts and bills, a lot of them with Leland's name on them. Plus some notes in my mother's handwriting."

Zane couldn't deny the surge of excitement he'd felt when he'd opened the case and seen the small stack of papers. He'd studied every bit of writing or print that he could see without touching anything.

"You're basically right. The bills and receipts are photocopies of Leland Hendricks's financial records. I can't read much of the handwritten notes, but it looks like Lou Ann was keeping a journal or a record of Leland's activities." He angled his head and spotted another familiar name. "And Donna's."

Anna started forward. "Well, take them out."

He glared at her. "I have to preserve the chain of evidence as much as possible. You're absolutely sure you didn't touch even one sheet of paper?"

She nodded.

"You'd swear under oath?"

She turned pale and her lower lip trembled, but she nodded. "Of course. I'm not lying."

Relief fluttered in his chest. "Good. That helps. I need to photograph the suitcase just as it is. Then I'll bag each piece of paper after I photograph it in place. I don't want any doubt that the papers are authentic and untouched."

He looked up in time to see Anna put a trembling hand to her head.

"You need to lie down. Get some sleep.

Tomorrow you're going back to Dallas. I'll arrange for a bodyguard for you until all this is over."

He skirted the table and put his arm around her waist. "Now come on. I can't have you fainting in the evidence room."

"I'm sorry," she mumbled.

Zane tightened his hold on her. Her firm yet supple waist and hips reminded him of her lovely body, naked and golden, beneath his. Despite the hour, despite his irritation with her, his body reacted.

Back in the break room, he lowered her gently to the couch.

She sighed and closed her eyes.

He turned out the light and stood there for a moment, watching her, torturing himself by letting the memory of their lovemaking push its way into his mind. He grew hard just from looking at her generous, luscious lips, her small, perfect breasts, the vee between her legs.

He gritted his teeth to keep from groaning out loud as he forced his brain to stop picturing her naked and uninhibited. He needed to get back to photographing and tagging the evidence Sarah had brought to Justice. It could mean a break in the case. He turned to go.

"Zane?" The soft voice pulled at his heart-strings.

"Yeah, honey?"

"You and your dad—"

Apprehension arrowed through his gut. Her voice was so quiet he could barely understand her. But he heard *your dad*.

He stepped over to the couch and perched on the edge near her thighs. "Annie, stop thinking about all this and go to sleep."

She reached out and caught his wrist, curling her fingers around it as far as they would go. "I know your dad hurt you. But tonight—he was with you tonight wasn't he?"

His heart pounded. He knew where she was going. He'd already been there and it had turned his whole attitude upside down.

She didn't wait for his answer. "He was there, with you, so he couldn't have been the one who attacked me."

"I know." Zane's voice sounded choked to his own ears.

"He's not the killer."

Zane couldn't have described how he felt at hearing the words he'd never dared to say to himself. Warring emotions threatened to pull him apart. He swallowed and clenched his jaw. It didn't matter if he was simultaneously relieved and terrified, confident and confused. His job was to *focus*.

He put his hand over hers. "The evidence is certainly pointing in a different direction."

"Damn it, Zane. Step away from your badge for a minute. Think like a son, not like a Texas Ranger. Your dad is a wonderful man. He loves you more than anything."

He cleared his suddenly clogged throat. That was the reason he couldn't let down his guard. Couldn't give in to his emotions. He was in charge. People depended on him to be brave, to be rational, to catch the killer—not to be crippled by emotion.

He stood. "Go to sleep," he said gruffly.

"What comes next?"

"I already told you what comes next. In the morning you're going back to Dallas."

"I don't want to leave—" She stopped. "This is my case, too."

"I can't be worrying about you. I've got to put all this evidence together and see if we can call a grand jury."

"Evidence against Leland?"

He nodded.

"So you believe your dad is innocent?"

Zane shrugged. "Who knows? But I don't have any evidence on him and I do on Leland. He tampered with the videotape the night of your mother's murder. Donna Hendricks destroyed his alibi for Sarah's time of death, although she may be lying out of hatred and resentment. And then there's whatever we find in your mom's papers. That's a lot of strikes against Leland."

"That's true." Anna sat up. "Zane, please. I need to stay here. Maybe if I see or speak to whoever attacked me, I can recognize him."

"No. That's out of the question. I want you away from here, out of the murderer's reach. If you died—" His throat seized.

She gave him a funny look. "You'd feel responsible?" She stood and looked up at him, her sleepy green eyes questioning.

He stepped closer and touched the edge of her bandage with his forefinger.

She caught her lower lip between her teeth.

"I'd feel," he whispered, sliding his hand around the back of her neck. He bent his head and kissed her, deeply, thoroughly.

Her arms wrapped around his neck as she returned his kiss.

Zane cursed himself for a fool as he lowered her to the couch. Still, at least for the rest of tonight, Anna would be safe.

## Chapter Thirteen

By the time Anna awoke the next morning, Zane had arranged for one of his Rangers to escort her back to Dallas. He'd walked her next door to the inn and told her to pack and be ready. She'd tried to protest again, but he was stronger this morning. He'd drawn on his determination and flatly told her he didn't need her here any longer.

He'd forced himself to ignore her look of surprised hurt, and left, making sure she locked her door behind him.

It was the right decision. Hell, it was a decision he should have made four days ago.

Whatever it was that made him crave her touch, that made him long to be with her, had to be squelched. Personal feelings had no place in a murder investigation. They were dangerous, distracting.

Early this morning, as he'd watched her sleep and felt her soft breath against his shoulder, he faced the hard truth.

It was his fault she'd nearly been killed last night. She shouldn't even have been here. He should have sent her back to Dallas that first night, after he'd taken her statement.

Now he sat at the sheriff's desk, forcing himself to concentrate on the evidence he'd collected. The most interesting and yet puzzling information were the papers Lou Ann had collected and kept.

From what he saw, the obvious conclusion was that she was planning to blackmail Leland—and Donna.

That information, along with the altered videotape and Donna's statement that she'd seen Leland sneaking out of his house on the night of Sarah's murder was enough to convene a grand jury.

Sitting back in his chair, Zane rubbed a weary hand over his face. It was also more than enough to exonerate his dad. His throat tightened and his eyes burned. What would this mean to his family? His mom, Sloan, his dad? Would it heal the wounds?

A peculiar longing settled deep inside him. He'd missed his dad.

He sat up, clearing his throat and composing his face. He needed to get going. He had a lot to do today. Picking up his cell phone, he punched in a familiar number.

"Hey, Bud," his brother Sloan said cheerily. Zane frowned and glanced at his watch. Usually, Sloan was asleep at nine o'clock in the morning if he wasn't on a case. Then he was grouchy until at least noon.

"Look, Squirt, I can't wait any longer. You've got to get here *today*."

"Don't get your shorts in a twist. I'm on my way."

"Where are you?"

"Throwing my bag in the car. It shouldn't take two hours."

"Right. The way you drive. Don't come yet. I need you to stay there. I've got some papers to give you, and I want to fill you in. I'll be there as soon as I make sure Anna's safely on her way back to Dallas."

"Anna?" Amusement and curiosity tinged his brother's voice. "The mousy little sister?"

"She's not mousy."

"Oh? So how'd you get so concerned about her?"

"Because she was almost killed last night, by whoever killed Lou Ann and Sarah."

"*Whoa.* Is she all right?"

"Yeah, but I'm making sure she's out of harm's way."

"So why come here? I can probably be there before your Anna leaves."

"I don't want anyone, even the deputies, to know about this. Besides, I'm going to convene a grand jury. I have ample evidence against Leland Hendricks."

"Hendricks? No kidding. You think he's the killer?"

"No. It doesn't feel right. I don't think Leland is clever enough or brave enough, but the evidence all points to him."

"It doesn't feel right because you still think Dad's guilty." Sloan's tone changed, turned cold.

"What I never got is why you always defended him."

"Because he's my dad."

Zane drew in a deep breath. "Dad didn't do it."

After a stunned pause, Sloan spoke. "Never thought I'd hear those words from you. What makes you so sure?"

"He was with me last night when the murderer tried to kill Anna."

"Okay, Bud. Looks like I'm going to need a lot of briefing."

"I'll be there in a couple of hours."

For an instant Sloan was silent. "Zane? It'll be good to see you."

Zane's eyes stung. "Yeah, Squirt. You, too."

WITHIN A HALF HOUR Zane stood in the doorway of the police station, watching the Ranger and Anna leave town. She hadn't spoken to him or even looked at him. She was hurt and angry, but right now he couldn't do anything about that.

He had to make sure Sloan had every bit of information he possessed before he turned the investigation over to him. He knew Sloan was one of the best. And he'd be able to inspire the townspeople's confidence more than Zane. After all, Sloan had been sheriff of Justice for five years.

It took him about twenty minutes to make sure he had everything he needed, including Leland's videotape, all the statements he'd gathered and Lou Ann's suitcase.

He thanked the deputies for their help and told them that Sergeant Sloan McKinney would be taking over the investigation.

Then he climbed into his car. But instead of heading for Dallas, he turned in the opposite direction, toward his parents' house.

It was only a couple of blocks to the street

where he'd grown up. As he pulled up to the house, he had to force himself not to peel away from the curb and head toward the Interstate.

He got out of his car and started up the sidewalk.

His dad rounded the corner of the house and paused, obviously surprised to see his son. He looked like he'd been working in the yard. His work pants sported grass stains and his tennis shoes were plastered with grass clippings. He took a cloth from his back pocket and wiped his face.

Zane swallowed as his dad stopped in front of him.

"Hey, Bud," Jim said. His face was lined with worry and his hand shook as he stuffed the cloth back into his pocket. "What's up?"

"Annie was attacked last night, while you were with me."

Jim's gaze darkened. "Is she all right?"

"Yeah, no thanks to me. Richie was a diversion, so they could get to Annie."

"You're awfully hard on yourself, Zane. Always have been."

Zane shrugged. A lump had erupted from somewhere and was lodged in his throat. It had probably been a bad idea to come here.

Right now he couldn't even say why he'd done it.

"Your mom's inside. She'll be glad to see you and feed you."

Zane smiled, then took a shaky breath. "Dad—"

Jim's expression turned wary and Zane felt a deep, suffocating shame for the way he'd treated his father all these years.

"Dad, I just wanted to say—"

"Bud, is it something about the case? Something about me?"

He shook his head. "No, it's me."

Jim frowned. "You? Are you hurt, son?"

This was the hardest thing Zane had ever done. And yet in a way it was also the most important.

"I'm sorry, Dad—" His voice failed him. He cleared his throat. "I've been an ass. Can you…can you forgive me?"

Jim McKinney's eyes filled with tears as he took a tentative step forward.

Zane reached out and hugged his dad, blinking to stop his own tears.

THE NEXT NIGHT Anna sat in the spacious living room of her apartment in her little red camisole and pajama bottoms, nursing a glass of wine and contemplating turning on the television.

She'd fixed dinner, just like she'd fixed breakfast and lunch, but most of it had gone uneaten. She'd always loved her apartment with its balcony looking out at the city of Dallas. But she'd been back hardly more than twenty-four hours, and it felt like a spacious, beautifully decorated prison.

It infuriated her that Zane McKinney had gotten to her. He was a stiff-necked, arrogant, emotionless man. There was nothing about him that appealed to her.

*Liar.*

Her mind fed her a slide show of his attributes—his even features, the smoky-blue eyes, that beautiful, sexy mouth. Not to mention his long, sleekly muscled body.

And those hands. Liquid desire swirled within her at the memory of his hands touching her.

"Fine," she muttered. "So he's gorgeous."

What about his cold determination? His ability to make exquisite love to her one moment and morph back into Zane McKinney, Texas Ranger, the next.

What an idiot she was, believing that their coupling had meant more to him than just a fling—a release of tension in a dangerous situation. In those blissful moments, she'd been sure she was seeing a side of him that he never showed. A tender, vulnerable side. The real man behind the badge.

But whatever she thought she'd seen always disappeared the next day or sometimes in the next instant. And she knew why. The fact remained that he hated her mother for destroying his family.

A horrible thought occurred to her. Had he screwed her and walked away out of revenge?

She stood and took her glass to the kitchen. She hadn't slept much last night and although she was drowsy, she still felt too keyed up to sleep. She yawned.

That was Zane's fault, too. She'd never been more comfortable, more content, than when she was lying on the lumpy break room couch with him, their bodies entwined on the narrow cushions.

Her eyes filled with tears and she wiped at them angrily.

*Get over yourself.* They had succumbed to a physical attraction that was enhanced by danger. That was all.

What was important was that her mother and sister were finally getting justice.

She turned off the lights and stepped over

to pull the drapes across the French doors to the balcony.

The doorbell rang.

She jumped and her heart began to pound. Nobody came to see her at this time of the night without calling first. She thought about Zane's insistence that she get out of Justice for her own safety. Could the killer have followed her?

She crept silently over to the door and peered through the peephole. Her heart bounced up into her throat. Her mouth went dry.

With shaking fingers she slipped the chain off the door and opened it.

"Hi," Zane said, looking sheepish and achingly handsome at the same time. He had on dress pants and a white shirt open at the collar.

Anna swallowed. "Hi," she croaked. "What…what are you doing here? Did something happen?"

He looked down at his boots then lifted his gaze to hers. "Can I come in?"

Her heart thundering in her ears, she stepped back and opened the door wider.

He walked in and stepped over to the French doors, his back to her. She studied him. His shoulders were tight, his hands were jammed in his pockets.

Anna closed the door and stood in front of it, wondering why he wasn't talking. Her brain raced with all the possible reasons he'd come here. Had Leland confessed? Had someone else been killed? Was he missing her as much as she missed him?

"Nice apartment," he said without turning around. He jingled the change in his pocket.

"Thank you…" She had no idea what to say. She'd never seen him like this. Tentative, almost shy.

"Zane? What is it?"

He turned, a small wary smile on his face.

"Why are you here?" She was beginning to be scared. "Is everything all right?"

"I don't know." He shrugged and ran a hand through his hair. "Annie—"

Her throat tightened. She'd started out hating that he called her Annie. She'd never let anyone call her that. Now she realized that she might have to live the rest of her life with that voice echoing in her ears.

"I don't know how to do this," he continued. "I've spent my life striving to be as unlike my father as I possibly could. But I think my real fear was that if I ever made a lifetime commitment to someone, I'd end up breaking it, just like him."

Anna stared at him. He was as nervous as a teenage boy on his first date. Despite her effort not to be hopeful, her heart fluttered like a girl with a crush.

His gaze moved over her face like a caress. Finally he frowned and looked down. "Well, you might want to know that your attacker came in through the bathroom window. We found a footprint on the sill." He moved toward the door, on his way out of her life.

She watched him as he walked past her, as his unmistakable scent wafted across her nostrils.

Her scalp burned with anger. If he thought he could come here and give her some lame excuse for his inability to make a commitment, he was dead wrong.

"Zane?" She reached out and caught his arm.

He stopped and angled his head without actually turning to look at her.

"You came all this way to tell me the murderer came in through the bathroom window?"

His jaw clenched. "And to make sure you were all right."

"I'm just fine. But you could have found

that out from your Ranger buddy who escorted me here." She sucked in courage with a lungful of air.

"This is not fair. You're going to make me take the risk, aren't you? You can face a killer but you can't handle one relatively small female?"

He raised his heather-blue eyes to hers, but he didn't speak. He looked both miserable and hopeful.

She took a deep breath. "Okay, then." She took his hands in hers. They were trembling.

"Zane McKinney, will you—" her breath caught "—marry me?"

"Marry me?" Zane said at the same time.

For a few seconds Anna stood there, wondering if what she'd seen and heard was real. She squeezed his hands.

He smiled at her, a big beautiful smile. "Well?" he said. "That wasn't so bad, was it?"

Unable to speak, she shook her head.

"Okay, then, what about your answer?" His smile faltered a little.

She swallowed. "What about yours?"

He slipped his hands from hers and pulled her close. "I guess this is how it's going to be. No matter what I do, you're going to be right there, aren't you?"

She grinned, even though her eyes were blurry with tears. "You bet. If we're in this at all, we're in it together."

He smiled, gazing down at her. "Okay, then, one, two, three—"

In unison, they said *yes*.

\* \* \* \* \*

*Find out how the investigation proceeds, and more about who may have attacked Sarah and Anna Wallace, when* TRACE EVIDENCE IN TARRANT COUNTY *by Delores Fossen, the second book in* THE SILVER STAR OF TEXAS *trilogy, debuts in February 2007.*

*Happily ever after is just the beginning...*

*Turn the page for a sneak preview of*
**DANCING ON SUNDAY AFTERNOONS**
*by*
*Linda Cardillo*

*Harlequin Everlasting—Every great love
has a story to tell.™*
*A brand-new line from Harlequin Books
launching this February!*

# *Prologue*

*Giulia D'Orazio*
1983

I had two husbands—Paolo and Salvatore.

Salvatore and I were married for thirty-two years. I still live in the house he bought for us; I still sleep in our bed. All around me are the signs of our life together. My bedroom window looks out over the garden he planted. In the middle of the city, he coaxed tomatoes, peppers, zucchini—even grapes for his wine—out of the ground. On weekends, he used to drive up to his cousin's farm in Waterbury and bring back manure. In the winter, he wrapped the peach tree and the fig tree with rags and black rubber hoses against the cold, his massive, coarse hands gentling those trees as if they were his fragile-skinned babies. My neighbor, Dominic Grazza, does that for me now. My boys have no time for the garden.

In the front of the house, Salvatore planted roses. The roses I take care of myself. They are giant, cream-colored, fragrant. In the afternoons, I like to sit out on the porch with my coffee, protected from the eyes of the neighborhood by that curtain of flowers.

Salvatore died in this house thirty-five years ago. In the last months, he lay on the sofa in the parlor so he could be in the middle of everything. Except for the two oldest boys, all the children were still at home and we ate together every evening. Salvatore could see the dining room table from the sofa, and he could hear everything that was said. "I'm not dead, yet," he told me. "I want to know what's going on."

When my first grandchild, Cara, was born, we brought her to him, and he held her on his chest, stroking her tiny head. Sometimes they fell asleep together.

Over on the radiator cover in the corner of the parlor is the portrait Salvatore and I had taken on our twenty-fifth anniversary. This brooch I'm wearing today, with the diamonds—I'm wearing it in the photograph also—Salvatore gave it to me that day.

Upstairs on my dresser is a jewelry box filled with necklaces and bracelets and earrings. All from Salvatore.

I am surrounded by the things Salvatore gave me, or did for me. But, God forgive me, as I lie alone now in my bed, it is Paolo I remember.

Paolo left me nothing. Nothing, that is, that my family, especially my sisters, thought had any value. No house. No diamonds. Not even a photograph.

But after he was gone, and I could catch my breath from the pain, I knew that I still had something. In the middle of the night, I sat alone and held them in my hands, reading the words over and over until I heard his voice in my head. I had Paolo's letters.

\* \* \* \* \*

*Be sure to look for*
*DANCING ON SUNDAY AFTERNOONS*
*available January 30, 2007.*
*And look, too, for our other*
*Everlasting title available,*
*FALL FROM GRACE by Kristi Gold.*

*FALL FROM GRACE*
*is a deeply emotional story*
*of what a long-term love really means.*
*As Jack and Anne Morgan discover,*
*marriage vows can be broken—*
*but they can be mended, too.*
*And the memories of their marriage*
*have an unexpected power to bring back*
*a love that never really left....*

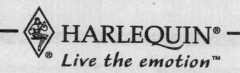

# HARLEQUIN®
# INTRIGUE®

## BREATHTAKING ROMANTIC SUSPENSE

Shared dangers and passions lead to electrifying romance and heart-stopping suspense!

Every month, you'll meet six new heroes who are guaranteed to make your spine tingle and your pulse pound. With them you'll enter into the exciting world of Harlequin Intrigue— where your life is on the line and so is your heart!

## THAT'S INTRIGUE—
## ROMANTIC SUSPENSE
## AT ITS BEST!

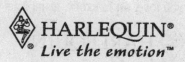

# HARLEQUIN®
## *Presents*

**The world's bestselling romance series...
The series that brings you your favorite authors,
month after month:**

Helen Bianchin...Emma Darcy
Lynne Graham...Penny Jordan
Miranda Lee...Sandra Marton
Anne Mather...Carole Mortimer
Susan Napier...Michelle Reid

**and many more uniquely talented authors!**

Wealthy, powerful, gorgeous men...
Women who have feelings just like your own...
The stories you love, set in exotic, glamorous locations...

# HARLEQUIN®
## *Presents*

**Seduction and Passion Guaranteed!**

HPDIR104

# HARLEQUIN

## Super Romance®

## ...there's more to the story!

Superromance.
A *big* satisfying read about unforgettable
characters. Each month we offer *six* very different
stories that range from family drama to adventure
and mystery, from highly emotional stories to
romantic comedies—and much more! Stories
about people you'll believe in and care about.
Stories too compelling to put down....

Our authors are among today's *best* romance
writers. You'll find familiar names and talented
newcomers. Many of them are award winners—
and you'll see why!

If you want the biggest and best
in romance fiction, you'll get it
from Superromance!

## Exciting, Emotional, Unexpected...

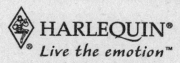

# HARLEQUIN®
### *Live the emotion*™